The Prodigal's Daughter

By Tasia Lawrence

Contents

Chapter 1

Paris

Detective Milan Brown sits at her desk facing her office window with a view of the city. Her hands cradle her head as her elbows rest on her desk. She closes her eyes and releases a slow exhale as she massages her temples to alleviate some tension before delving into her newest assignment. Milan grabs a file folder stamped with the word "confidential" across the middle in bold, red ink. The name "David" is typed on the file tab. She gazes at the closed folder for a few moments because this case is personal. She inserts the folder into a manila envelope and places it inside a drawer on the side of her desk and locks it. She picks up another file on her desk with the name "Paris" on the file tab and walks out of the office.

Milan pulls up to a seedy run-down part of town. The buildings are dilapidated, and it's evident the town had been forsaken long ago. She parks across the street from a partially exposed building. She checks her surroundings and opens the file folder labeled "Paris" revealing a closeup photo of a young woman wearing a tank top. She closes the folder and places it in her shoulder bag on the passenger side floor. Milan checks the clip of her firearm and places it in her shoulder holster. She pulls a smaller pistol out of her dashboard and secures it to her ankle holster.

A partially demolished building is in her line of sight. The building has several openings due to a lack of maintenance and wear, enabling her to see right through to the back of the property. She looks around her immediate area before walking into one of the openings in the building. A man wearing a suit is standing inside watching her. He waits until she notices him before walking away briskly. Milan is stunned. She rushes in the man's direction.

"David? David! Dad?"

Milan yells, her voice shakes when she calls the man dad.

The man picks up the pace. Milan runs behind him, following him down a descending hallway to the lower level of the building. Before she enters the hallway, she spots a black jeep driving slowly in her front view.

"Milan, if you see a black jeep, you'd better take cover! Get down now!"

Gunfire pierces the air around her. She ducks and scurries down the hallway. She spots the man running down a hall lit by daylight through a window. He makes a sharp turn around a corner and Milan follows. He runs through a doorway leading outside to the back of the building. A black car waits with the back passenger side door open, and he hops in.

"Don't worry they're after me. They don't remember you. 427 Willowbrook Cove! I'll explain everything."

David says before shutting the door. Milan chases the vehicle, but it speeds off before she can make contact.

Milan steps outside behind the car and memorizes the license plate number. She assesses her surroundings as she draws her weapon. She stays close to the side of the building and turns the corner. The sound of banging draws Milan's attention to the other side of the lot in the opposite direction. As soon as Milan retraces her steps and passes the doorway the heel of her shoe gets stuck inside of a hole in the ground. She holsters her gun as she tries to regain her balance. Before she can secure her weapon, the ground gives way and she falls into a hole, landing on a set of stairs.

Milan blacks out for a few minutes. The sound of metal rattling helps her regain consciousness. She opens her eyes and rolls over on her back in pain. She pinpoints the location of the noise. There is a door with a bolted lock a few feet away from where she is laying. Milan locates her firearm nearby, so she whimpers through the pain as she carefully stands to her feet. She grabs her firearm and holds it at her side. The light peering in from the top of the stairwell illuminates the room. Milan is in the cellar of the building. Beyond the staircase is a long corridor. Milan stands in place and surveilles the area. Through the flicker of light from a bulb on the ceiling a door is visible at the end of the hall. She quietly approaches the door in front of her with the bolted lock and knocks lightly.

Moaning and the sound of chains rattling activates Milan's detective instincts. She looks down at her pistol and contemplates shooting off the lock. To avoid injuring anyone she looks around the immediate area for something to pry the lock open.

A shadow from the top of the stairs dims the light and the room darkens. Heavy footsteps charge down the stairs. Milan takes cover behind a large crate under the stairs. She peeks around the crate to get a clear view of the man. A tall stocky man with disheveled hair rushes to the bolted door with a ring of keys and unlocks the door. Chains rattle aggressively as gagged moans fill the air. Milan stands to her feet with her pistol at her side. The man pokes his head out of the doorway and looks down the hall. Milan stops in place and is shielded by a beam behind the stairs. She pulls out her cell phone and sends a text message to her unit supervisor alerting her about a potential hostage situation. She turns her phone on silent mode and places it back in her pocket. She pulls her weapon close to her chest with her finger on the trigger and walks along the wall leading up to the open door. The muffled sounds grow louder before suddenly a young woman cries out.

"I don't know what happened! I was in here chained to this pipe and the door was locked, how could I possibly know what's going on behind this door!"

"The front door is broken, and someone has been down here. What did you hear beyond the door, Paris?"

Milan stops in her tracks when she hears Paris' name. She increases her stride and peeks into the room. The shabbily dressed man stands before a young woman while holding a long blunt object in his hand. The woman is half dressed and cuffed to a pipe against the wall. A thick piece of cloth used to gag her dangles around her neck. Paris looks thin and malnourished. She looks up at the man in terror. The man stands in place while looking around the room. Paris glances at Milan peeking from the side of the doorway. Her eyes grow bigger, but she quickly shifts her focus to the man to avoid bringing attention to Milan.

The man begins to walk to other end of the small room, still in search of something. Milan seizes the opportunity to subdue the large man. She draws her weapon and points it at the back of his head.

"Don't you dare move!"

Milan proclaims as she unhooks her hand cuffs from her waist holster. Surprised by Milan's presence the man flinches as he turns his head slightly to size up his opponent. He raises his hands slowly and catches a glimpse of Milan's small frame from her shadow on the wall. Milan orders the man to put his hands behind his head. The man complies and watches her through the corner of his eye. Paris looks on with worry in her eyes as she tries to squeeze her wrist through her cuffs to break free. As soon as Milan secures one of the cuffs the man yanks the cuff forward, grabs her arm, and flips her over his shoulder. He slams Milan to the floor and attempts to restrain her with her cuffs. Milan is dizzy and fights to remain conscious before this battle leads to a tragic ending for her and Paris. Paris screams as she aggressively yanks the cuffs against the pipe in an attempt to break the cuffs or the pipe. Milan uses the man's weight as leverage to shift her legs forward and she kicks him in the groin with all her might. The man is stunned, and his eyes widen. He maintains a tight hold onto Milan's arm while grabbing his groin with his other hand. Milan is in a tug of war with the man as she tries to reach her pistol a few feet away. Paris is in the background kicking the pipe at the connection point so she can slip the cuff chain through.

The man has regained some of his strength and his pain dies down and he is seething in anger. Milan grabs his arm to pull her weight closer to him and swiftly kicks the man in the face. She breaks his nose, and he loosens his grip on Milan's arm as he falls to the floor unconscious. Milan grabs the man by his shoulders, drags him across the room and cuffs his arms behind his back around a pillar. She searches the man's pockets until she finds his keys. She tries each key on the ring until one matches the cuffs on Paris' wrists. Milan sends a call for the officers in her unit to come to the scene. Milan and Paris wait upstairs on the ground level for her squad unit to arrive.

Sergeant Laura Simon is the first to arrive on the scene. As she walks toward Milan and Paris, she wears a look of disappointment. Milan picks up on Simon's countenance but decides not to address her suspicions in the moment. Sergeant Simon walks over to Paris and Paris quickly puts her head down, looking away from Simon. Additional officers arrive at the scene and Milan points them in the direction of the culprit in the lower level. Milan stands to the side and observes facial expressions and body language. A few of the officers exit their vehicle visibly angered at the sight of Paris. Milan must think quickly if she wants answers. She sits beside Paris and observes her body language before speaking. Paris keeps her head low but periodically looks up at the approaching officers. Milan is mindful of how Paris' body language changes with each officer and who she may be familiar with. Milan puts her arm around Paris and speaks quietly.

"We need to get out of here ok, and I'm going to need you to trust me."

Milan says with a smile to confuse the other officers. Milan nudges Paris' elbow, motioning for her to stand. They quickly walk out of the parking lot and around the corner towards Milan's car.

"Brown! She can't leave the scene. She needs to be taken in for questioning. We'll take it from here, detective."

A male officer says as he walks toward the ladies with his hand on his weapon. They both turn around as they continue to walk. His body language shows his preparedness to act and subdue the women. Milan draws her weapon and points it at the opposing officer. She tells Paris to walk behind her and to keep going.

"Stand down, Jacobs! Take your hand off your weapon."

Jacobs complies reluctantly. Milan and Paris pick up the pace and make it to the car. They get in as Milan keeps her weapon pointed and Jacobs. They drive off and head to 427 Willowbrook Cove.

Milan turns off her cell phone and makes a stop along the way. Since Milan was a little girl, her father always told her to keep a small office or studio that no one knows anything about, and to use a different cell phone in the area. About thirty minutes away from the crime scene, Milan pulls into an alley surrounded by commercial buildings. She presses a button on the ceiling of her car hidden underneath the fabric. A garage door opens, Milan looks around her immediate environment and pulls into a large, open space. The space is reminiscent of a former mechanics garage with a small office and reception window on one side and offices that have been sealed off on the other. The floors are clean beige marble, and the place is empty.

Milan looks over at Paris who is curled up in a deep sleep with her head resting on the window. Milan calls out to Paris, and she is startled out of her sleep. She hands her a sweatshirt from her backseat and tells her everything will be ok, but they must keep moving.

"You're Milan, right?"

Paris asks. Milan nods. Paris pulls a note from her pocket and hands it to Milan.

"I found this at the 1st place I was being held. I woke up with blood on my hand, I guess that's my thumb print. Maybe you were next."

The note reads, Paris, Milan, Lille, Marseille with a blood-stained thumb print next to Paris' name.

Chapter 2

Milan

Ten Years Ago

Milan excitedly walks through her new college campus. She finds a cozy spot under a weeping willow tree and sits on the cool grass. She is inspired by the architecture and the array of greenery and colorful flowers around the campus. She remembers the art supply pack she received during orientation earlier in the day. Beaming from ear-to ear, she pulls out her sketchbook and starts sketching the cherry blossom tree a few feet away. The bit of light peering through the low hanging tree is shadowed completely as someone approaches.

"Milan Brown!"

A firm voice says coming from Milan's left side. Milan is startled. She looks out of the corner of her eye before turning completely. A man wearing a black suit and dark shades holds out a cell phone with a video on the screen.

"Who are you?"

Milan asks, suspicious.

The man repeats himself and insists she confirm her recognition of the man in the video. It's her father, David seemingly strung out on drugs inside a janky room. Milan remains silent and quickly packs her belongings.

"I'm going to need you to come with us."

The man says, firmly. Milan positions herself in a squat position as she discreetly observes her surroundings. She is new to campus and is unsure of the closest exits. There is one North from her current location. This exit leads to the street off campus, a train station is nearby as well as a busy intersection. The student parking garage where her car is parked is about a half of a mile south and may be too far to outrun this extremely fit man. She looks at the video and gives the false perception that she is trying to find recognition in the man's face. A couple of students exit the student center. She makes a run for it. Full speed ahead to the closest exit and does not look back. Milan hops the fence and keeps running across the street and into the train station. She can hear the train coming as she approaches the station. She picks up the pace and runs down the stairs, hops the turnstile and makes it inside the train just as the doors close. The sound of heavy steps running down the steps sends Milan into panic mode. The train pulls off, she walks in between the connecting train cars and enters one of the cars through the emergency door. Milan slams the door behind her and leans against it. She exhales a sigh of relief. The train car is empty. Milan turns around and looks through the windows leading to the connecting doors. There are a few people scattered throughout the train, nothing out of the ordinary.

She reaches her stop, which is a five-minute walk to her mother's home. She exits the train and is relieved that she is almost home to safety. A man dressed similar to the one on her campus steps in her path. He studies her briefly before quickly pistol whipping her, striking the bridge of her nose and she blacks out.

Present Day

After gazing at the note for a few moments and taking a trip down memory lane, Milan looks up at Paris and is unsure if she did the right thing in bringing her to her secret hideout. No one else in the world knows about Milan's spot and her security may have been breached.

A knock on the garage door startles both Paris and Milan. Milan draws her weapon and steps out of the vehicle. She views the camera footage on her phone to get a glimpse of the person standing outside. A letter slides through a slit under the garage door. A man wearing sunglasses and a ski mask looks directly into the camera and mouths "it's from David" and walks away. Milan removes a note from the envelope.

"If I can find you, they can track you. It must be the girl. They may be tracking you through Paris. Check for chips under the skin. There will be a helicopter waiting for you on the roof of the glass building East of yours. Be there in an hour. Don't drive, walk. Dad."

Milan walks over to the passenger side of the car. The door is open, and Paris is gone. Milan checks the video footage through her phone and spots Paris jumping out of a window on the second level. Milan walks across the large garage space to a door behind a curtain. Beyond the door is a narrow hallway with sensor lights that light her path as she walks through. On her left is a hidden door. The door blends seamlessly with the wall and can only be found if you know where to look. Milan checks the surrounding area through her video footage connected to her cell. The coast is clear, so she steps outside and closes the door behind her. Once closed, the door is camouflaged within the stucco siding seamlessly.

What Milan cannot see is a series of closed-circuit cameras strategically stationed in the corners of the buildings surrounding her hideout. Milan runs through the alley surrounded by other commercial buildings. When she gets closer to the street, she spots

Paris running up a long set of stairs. A black jeep turns the corner and speeds just as Milan crosses the street. She narrowly makes it to the curb as the jeep zips by. Milan is startled but not surprised, her father's warning was in alignment with her hunch about wanting to move to a new location on the outskirts of the city. Milan memorized the license plate number before the jeep sped around the corner. With Paris running up the stairs, still in sight, Milan leaps up the stairs, skipping a few steps as she goes. They are both out of breath when Milan reaches Paris. Milan grabs her arm firmly. Paris attempts to pull away, but she is no match for Milan's military trained strength.

"Wait! A chip. Did they put a chip under your skin?"

Milan asks through her heavy breathing.

Paris looks at her left thumb. She pulls her hand closer to her face and spots a small slit on the side of her thumb. She remembers waking up to someone stamping a piece of paper in blood with her thumb. She and Milan examine her thumb and look up at one another and it is clear what needs to be done.

"We have to get that chip out of there. They've been tracking us through you. They know where we are."

"Who are you? Aren't you one of them?" Paris says in confusion.

"I thought we were on the same team but, searching for you proved that they have different motives. I don't know what's going on but I'm going to find out. And it won't be the last thing I do."

Milan pulls a pocketknife out of her pocket and looks to Paris for a response. Paris looks away and tells Milan to "just do it." Milan pulls an alcohol pad from her jacket pocket and presses down on Paris' finger feeling for a foreign object. She wipes Paris' finger then the knife. Milan tells Paris to gather the bottom of her shirt and to bite down on it. Paris complies and closes her eyes bracing herself for impact. Milan presses the edge of the knife into the faint slit on her finger. Paris moans in agony as Milan applies pressure to force the chip out. After a few seconds a small, square silver metal colored microchip protrudes from Paris' thumb. Milan takes a photo of the chip before crushing it on the ground with a rock.

Milan tells Paris to keep her wound wrapped in her shirt until it can be cleaned and treated. Milan leads Paris up the stairs and inside the lobby of a large building to travel through to the other side. Milan surveilles their surroundings to ensure they are not being followed. They reach a set of double doors leading outside when the black jeep approaches. Instinctively, the pair take cover on either side of the walls closest to the doors. The jeep rides slowly but never stops. As soon as the vehicle is out of sight, they cross the street and head toward the glass building.

The entrance is filled with security and a few plain clothes officers Paris recognizes.

"No, we can't go in there, not this way."

Paris says with fear in her voice. Milan nudges Paris to walk toward a side door that has been left cracked open. Inside on the right is a staircase ascending and another set descending. Straight ahead there is a doorway leading to a kitchen followed by a set of swinging doors leading out into the building lobby. They take a chance and travel up the stairs and hope it leads to the roof and not a dead end. They climb ten flights of stairs before reaching the fire exit to the roof. They hear talking outside the door. The talking is coming from a distance. Milan instructs Paris to wait inside while she checks things out. Beyond the door is a short black partition. Milan draws her weapon and peeks around the wall. The helicopter has landed and rests on a helipad with two men talking, frustrated. There is a plain clothed officer with his hand resting on his gun in his waist holster along with the pilot. Milan motions for Paris to come outside and they quietly walk around the door in the opposite direction of the wall. They both peek around the wall and the pilot spots Milan.

"Okay I'll go, that's fine. But I need you to stand at least fifty feet back, so I have room to take off."

The officer obliges and Milan and Paris hide until
the officer is near the door. The pilot boards and leaves
the door open. He gives Milan a nod and she and Paris
run as fast as they can to the helicopter and don't look
back. They board just as gun shots ring out. Milan
points her weapon at her fellow officer and shoots
back, purposely missing him.

"This isn't over, Brown!" He yells as he rushes back
through the door and out of sight.

Milan shuts the helicopter door, leans back, and
rests her head on her seat and closes her eyes.

Ten Years Ago

Milan wakes up in a cold sweat. She lay on her side
stuck in place wiggling her arms and legs to loosen the
grip of the ropes binding her ankles and wrists
together. She used the blanket on the bed to wipe the
warm liquid streaming down her face. She looks down
at a small pool of blood streaming from her nose. In a
panic Milan frantically rolls around the bed trying to
break free. Multiple sets of feet gallop down the stairs
toward Milan, so she freezes, closes her eyes and fake
sleep.

"She bled out a lot. Is she still breathing."

Two men stand before her, looking over her still body. One of the men bends down near her face. As his presence draws near Milan peeks out of her right eye, closest to the bed and holds her breath. The man places a mirror under nose to check her breathing. When the mirror doesn't fog, he checks the pulse on her neck.

"Her heart is beating, she's still alive. Let's go!"

To Milan's surprise the man scoops her up, one arm under the back of her neck and the other under her legs. Milan is mortified but, remains still and fights the urge to tense up and allows her body to go limp. Milan watches their steps through her squinted view. Since it was still daylight Milan estimates she had been unconscious only a few hours so, she couldn't be too far from home. The man with free hands pops the trunk and places Milan inside.

"No, TomRoy. In the backseat. We need the trunk empty."

TomRoy stops to think about whether to comply and after a few moments lays Milan on the back seat of the sedan. TomRoy gets into the passenger seat while the man giving instruction drives. Milan discreetly works on breaking free. After driving for a few minutes, they run into some commotion ahead and the car slows down.

"Let's just go around this mess, the highway shouldn't be far."

TomRoy grows frustrated as they are forced to come to a complete stop.

"No, the highway is just two blocks up. If we go around it'll take too long. Once we get on the highway there no stops for miles, we'll be off the grid and will be there in no time."

The news sends Milan into a panic. The ropes around her wrists are now loose but, she keeps her arms folded behind her back. A loud voice draws closer as they inch up to the intersection. There is a woman standing in the middle of the crosswalk yelling a message to passersby.

"He is coming soon! Repent, for the kingdom of Heaven is at hand. Everything we've done has been recorded in Heaven by the Father. Repent from your sinful ways while there is still time. God is love but, He is holy, and we are not, we need salvation through Jesus Christ. Even if you are a good person. We are born in sin and shaped in iniquity, our souls need salvation, for they will live on. Jesus is the only way to the Father. Search out a matter for yourself. The kingdom of heaven is at hand. God Loves you all so much. Learn of Him while there's still time!"

A clean woman tall in stature and well-dressed holds a sign that reads 'God is love, read about Him'. She walks slowly across the crosswalk and turns the sign in both directions so all incoming traffic can read her sign. TomRoy and the driver are so engrossed with the woman they hadn't noticed Milan completely free herself from bondage. The car comes to a complete stop. While on her side, Milan studies the door and is relieved to see a manual door lock. She pulls the door handle and the manual lock simultaneously. Without taking a second look she opens the door and runs as fast as she can in the opposite direction and across the street. Milan's stride is halted when a bullet pierces through her right calf. The driver has put the car in park and is in position to take another shot at Milan through his window. She falls to her knees but, the round of bullets flying past her head give her momentum to push past the pain and keep going.

Milan limps on her good leg and finds cover in between cars as she stumbles up the residential block. Milan checks on her wound and the sight of her calf and foot completely covered in blood makes her queasy. She tries to fight her dizziness to avoid fainting. She spots a truck in the shade and musters up the last of her energy to take cover beneath the bumper, where she blacks out.

The woman with the sign has crossed the street and traffic begins pouring in on the opposite side of the street. TomRoy and the driver's car is stuck in place for the time being. They ditch the car, the driver with his pistol in his hand, and they run across the street. They zip through oncoming traffic, narrowly avoiding being hit. TomRoy points to a trail of blood in the sidewalk. The driver is thrilled to follow the breadcrumbs leading to Milan. They follow the trail of blood to a black pickup truck where the trail ends. Milan is gone. Their hunt comes to an end when the sound of police sirens fills the air. They rush back to their vehicle and head toward the freeway.

Three days later Milan wakes up in a sterile white room. She lay on a hospital bed wearing medical pajamas and covered with a blanket. She pulls the blanket back to check on her leg. She was in so much pain she was certain her whole leg would be gone. Her leg is bandaged and clean down to her new white socks. She turns to her right and nearly jumps out of her skin. Her father is sitting at her bedside patiently waiting for her to notice his presence. He looks scruffy and tired. His countenance is worrisome and it's clear he is harboring secrets. Milan has managed to work with her dad's elusive behavior, just happy to see him when she can catch him. Although, she feels in her gut that there is more than what she's been hearing about her father's current mental state.

"I'm glad you're ok, Milan. I'll always be around, even if you can't always see me. I'll always protect you, for as long as I'm alive."

"I know dad. I'm glad you're ok too.

Milan is not satisfied with her father's vague response, this time.

"Where do you go when you're not around?

David gets up from his seat and leaves the room. He returns with a wheelchair and pulls it up to Milan's bedside. He reaches for her hand, and she allows him to help her into the chair. He tells her he wants to show her something as he wheels her out of the room. Just a few feet away from the room, they enter a three-car garage. The garage door ascends as they enter, revealing a woodsy landscape with fog-covered mountains on the horizon.

"Some place you have never been, because you were never here, ok."

Milan looks up at David in confusion but remains silent. David continues to look out onto the horizon.

"I just need you to trust me even though you don't know everything that's going on. Trusting me is for the best……For your safety."

David kneels to face Milan. He shares the potential for rumors about his character potentially distorting her view. "Nothing is what it seems", He says. "Believe half of what you see and none of what you hear." David offers clues about why she was captured but

remains as vague as possible. Milan knows her father
is hiding something. Even though she led him to
believe she has accepted his cryptic explanation, she
looks down at her wounds and is determined to avoid
losing her life over her father's secrets.

Milan tells her father that she would like to lie down
and rest. He wheels her back to her room and helps
her back into the bed. He kisses her on her forehead
and leaves the room. A few minutes pass and Milan
climbs back into the wheelchair. Before leaving the
room, she listens at the open doorway to pinpoint
movement in the house. The house is silent. She
wheels down the hall just as her father walks past the
front door at the end of the hall. He is on a phone call
and is facing the opposite direction. Milan stops
abruptly in fear that she will be seen. When her father
is out of sight, she wheels into the first open doorway
along her path on the right. Milan enters a large foyer
surrounded by floor to ceiling windows with views of
wooded land in the backyard. The foyer leads to
various parts of the house. A set of glass stairs leading
to the upper and lower levels is on her right, the
kitchen on her far right and a dark hallway in the right
corner. Milan is drawn to light peering through a black
door on a black wall straight ahead. She looks through
the window on her left to check on her father's
whereabouts. She can't see him, but she can hear him
on his phone call, so she makes a beeline for the room
and stops at the door. She looks up at the dome

security camera in the right corner above the door and decides to proceed through the door anyway.

Milan pushes the door open, and wheels herself into the office surrounded by windows with a view of the ocean beyond a field of grass. Milan closes the door behind her, leaving it cracked. The walls are covered in photos. Photos that tell a story of her parents' life, a life she knew nothing about. She wheels closer to the wall on her right and studies a photo of her mother wearing a black leotard with a skirt and ballet slippers standing on pointe. Another photo is of Milan sitting on her father's lap as a toddler attending one of her mother's ballet recitals. Milan in astonished. She never knew her mother was a dancer, nor does she remember attending a recital featuring her mother's work. Milan backs away from the wall, her wheelchair bumps into a file cabinet causing something to rattle behind it. She looks outside the door before reaching behind the cabinet to retrieve what was causing the noise. She pulls out a black plastic accordion file folder. Inside are multiple passport books featuring her father's picture with different alias's. The United States, Italy, France, and the United Kingdom. Also, newspaper clippings of events surrounding different landmarks in each country. She replaces the contents and puts the folder back behind the cabinet.

Milan wheels herself to a large black wooden desk near the window. She quickly opens the drawers attached to the desk. She was eager to find out more about her parents and their lives before she was born. She stumbles upon a folder labeled S.A.C. and opens the folder revealing a letter from the United States Military, Special Activities Center Division. The letter is addressed to David Brown with the acronym PMOO next to his name.

Footsteps draw near to the window outside. Milan hurriedly shoves the folder back into the drawer and scurries out of the room. She spots David walking back inside the house through the front door, so she wheels herself up to the nearest window in the seating area in the foyer. David notices Milan is not in her room, so he comes through the main house looking for her. He spots Milan then looks around the room and notices his office door wide open. David stands in the doorway for a while watching Milan, reading her body language, and observing any changes in her countenance. His private office is filled with secrets, secrets that may change her outlook on her parents and may cause an identity crisis learning about their past lives and activities. Milan can feel her father's presence but keeps her attention stayed on the view of the window.

David offers to fix Milan something to eat before her ride arrives to take her back to her mother's home. Milan is eager to get back home to research her findings and begin her investigation into her parents' secret lives. She agrees to eat something but tells David she would like to get dressed first.

"Down the hall to the right. You'll find some things you can fit."

David says pointing down the hall near his office as he's chopping vegetables for a couple of sandwiches. Milan looks at David suspiciously and wheels herself toward the dark hall. She finds a light switch on the wall. The view of the hallway caused a rush of emotion to fill Milan's body. A familiar cocktail of emotions, fear, anxiety, and joy come over Milan. She runs her hands along the wall as she travels down to the last door on the left. She opens the door to a bedroom that had been converted into a walk-in closet. Rosewood shelves cover every wall in the room. Floor to ceiling windows fill the room with light and provide a 180-degree view of the bare woods behind the home. Milan wheels herself to the bare shelves and opens the drawers. She rummages through the winter clothing in search of evidence revealing the owner or anything else to solve this puzzle she had awoken to.

Beneath the piles of neatly folded sweaters and sweatshirts Milan finds a tiny sweater reminiscent of the holidays. Red and black knit with snowflakes woven into the front. She pulls the sweater close to face and the scent brings her to stillness. Something familiar, the scent, the feel, memories of sitting across from a fire pit making smores and drinking hot cocoa flash through her mind. She knows she has been here before, but a clear memory of this place is out of her reach. David is unwilling to divulge anything about their lives in the past and wants her to forget she was even here. Milan rolls up the sweater and tucks it in the seat of her chair. She finds a taupe sweatsuit in her size and changes quickly. Milan wheels to the end of the hall and her father is out of sight. Two neatly made sandwiches have been left on a plate on the counter with two cups of orange juice. She grabs a plate and a cup of juice and pulls up to a small round table near a window.

Milan finishes her lunch and heads back to her room. She reaches the hall to find David standing outside near the front door. He is carrying crutches and has a jacket draped over his arm. When he locks eyes with Milan, he opens the door to the back seat. Milan receives the gesture and realizes that it is time for her to leave. She wheels slowly toward her father and tries to read his body language. Her father is usually reticent with his emotions and can give a mean poker face. David meets her at the door with the crutches and walks with her to the car door. He helps her into the car, and she is greeted by David's personal driver. David gets in on the other side and sits beside Milan. He extends his hand and Milan places her hand in his. David pats Milan's hand and tells her everything will be alright. Milan places her other hand on top of his and waits. She waits for more information, and explanation, some clarity. Something to reassure their safety. They ride along a path in the woods in silence.

Within a few minutes they pull up to a helipad at the center of the property. There is a helicopter waiting and a pilot in the cockpit. Milan is surprised at, yet another secret having been uncovered about her father. She looks at David with concern hoping for an explanation. David looks at Milan and can feel her disappointment through the glare in her eyes.

"One day it will all make sense, for now you're just going to have to trust me. This is your ride for the rest of the way home. It's safer this way."

David says to Milan as he points to the helicopter. Milan's eyes well with tears as she tries to speak.

"I don't even know you, David. What else are you hiding and why. Tell me the truth, now!"

"David? I'm your father, I'm not David to you, Milan."

David replies calmly yet firm.

"I've set you and your mother up in a high-rise apartment. My friend here will take you straight to the roof of your building. I put all the information you need in here."

David hands Milan a cell phone.

"Your unit number as well as a barcode fob to enter the building and the front door of your unit is in this phone. The code to access this phone is you and your mother's birthday. My cell number is in here as well, call me whenever you need me. I'll always be around even when you don't see me."

Milan accepts the phone despite her confusion. Although distant, David has always taken care of Milan and her mother and has shown up in the nick of time in moments of trouble.

Milan puts the cell phone in her pocket and David walks around to her side to help her out of the truck. They walk to the center of the helipad. The landing space is surrounded by naked trees, yet perfectly hidden from view from the outside. Milan scans the area to get an idea of the state or city she's in. Half a mile beyond the forest, directly behind the helicopter is the ocean. There are four large bodies of water in Milan's home state and two in the neighboring state. Milan looks up at her father and smiles.   In her mind she is closer than she has ever been to finding out who this stranger is beside her.

Chapter 3

Present Day

Milan and Paris have been traveling by air for about an hour. Milan opens her eyes as the helicopter descends into a wooded area. Memories begin to flood her mind about the last time she saw her father before running from her earlier today. They land on a helipad at the center of a cleared wooded area. The trees are plush, and the dark green leaves shield the helipad and their landing completely. Milan hurriedly de boards and Paris follows. Milan and Paris follow the asphalt covered path to her father's home. David walks out of the home and meets the ladies with a wide smile. Although it has been nearly ten years since she saw her father, Milan is overjoyed to see him alive and well.

Rumor has it, David has had a long-standing battle with drug addiction. Periodically, Milan would receive photos of her father in drug houses strung out. The photos and random tips were always sent anonymously. After a few years of his absence and knowledge of his personal struggles David's family would refer to him as the prodigal. Milan has been deeply disturbed by the family's lack of concern and empathy for David. Little effort has been made to seek help for David or at the very least a wellness check. Milan took matters into her own hands. She would set out on well-planned trips around the city to locate her father but, once her mother learned of her plans, she forbade her to continue. Milan and her father always had secret codes shared between the two of them, so Milan was on the lookout to decipher any subliminal messages sent from David. In one of the photos sent, David was slumped over a cushion on the floor of a rundown home seemingly strung out. He was winking slightly and formed a slight "ok" sign with his fingers. Milan knew in that moment her father was letting her know he was ok. She never knew what her father did for a living, but he always had access to funds, and they were well off. She figured David was on some top-secret mission to save the world, somehow. At least that's what she tells herself.

David and Milan embrace as Milan rests her head on her father's shoulder and squeezes him tight as he chuckles through the pain from the squeeze. David lifts his head and is delighted to see Paris. Milan and Paris are shocked when David calls Paris by name.

"I'm so glad you're both here, I have so much to share with you. It's time for you to learn everything, Milan."

They walk inside and enter a small room in the foyer. The house has is different from the last time

Milan was there a decade ago. An additional wall was added to the foyer creating a long narrow office on the left side of the foyer. They all face one another as they sit at a large black conference table in the middle of the room surrounded by black chairs on wheels. The sun shines bright through the large windows in the room.

David sits down across from the ladies and gets right to the point.

"Have either of you wondered why you're both named after cities in Europe."

Paris and Milan look at one another blankly. David shares a story about four colleagues, turned friends who were forced on a mission to preserve treasures from the earth that were hidden in plain sight. These treasures can be destructive if not handled properly and offer security for generations to come. Milan and Paris sit in confusion and wait for David to decipher his coded speech. David hesitates as he prepares the big reveal.

David pulls out a folder and spreads a collection of photos out on the table before the ladies. Surveillance, evidence of high-level foul play, including photos of Paris, Milan and two other girls when they were children. Photos of Paris and Mian at school, the playground, and out with their parents leading up to adulthood. Milan and Paris both spread the photos around the table, horrified that their every move had been documented.

"Who are the other girls in the photo?" Milan asks, frustrated.

"That's Lille and Marseille. Their fathers also work for the U.S military. We're Paramilitary Operations Officers, Special Activities Division."

Both Paris and Milan stare at David in silence.

"That's CIA, Milan. That's why I've been so secretive over the years, to protect you and your mother. Your father too Paris."

Paris and Milan look at one another and back at David.

"Once our opposition discovered we have daughters, they've had their eyes on the four of you. They were going to use you to get to us, that's why we kept you all at a distance. For a while they didn't know we had families. For years I was under cover on the streets trying to find these guys. I was living in crack and meth houses usually housed by other veterans trying to get information. I went through the whole rehab process and everything trying to discover their identities."

Paris and Milan question David about the sudden reveal of information. David informs Milan that had they not escaped from their captors they would have been tortured for information and killed. For over a decade they lost track of the girls but since Milan enlisted in the military and then joined the force their identities were uncovered.

Despite David's sudden openness Milan is still suspicious about David's motive. She asked David how he was able to find her at the drop of a hat. David sits down and reluctantly reveals to Milan his personal mode of surveillance of her life.

"Take off your right shoe and put your foot on the table. You too Paris."

"What? Why?!"

Paris and Milan say in unison.

"Just do it, I have to show you something."

Paris doesn't budge but wears a look of disdain and waits to see what Milan will do. After a few moments of defiance Milan complies. David turns off the light and pulls the shades down on the windows. He pulls out an infrared flashlight and shines it in front of her big toe. Milan and Paris are mortified to see a small square chip inside Milan's toe. Paris immediately tosses her shoe and sock to the side and puts her big toe in front of the light. Paris and Milan are mortified. The ladies yell at David in unison demanding answers.

Amidst the yelling David shares that he had the chip placed in Milan's toe when she was five years old. She wouldn't have remembered because she was under anesthesia. There is a group of opposing forces who are after something that they know is hidden with the four girls. Along with a location tracker there is a map and coordinates to places around the world that need to be safe guarded.

"You weren't supposed to know about this until after we were all gone."

David shares with a look of worry. Something Milan had never seen in her father. David has always had a can-do attitude and handled business and conflict effortlessly. David is being hunted and he wants to prepare the daughters to subdue and defeat the enemy. The group is known as legion because they are mighty and there are many members. David instructs the ladies to find Marseille and Lille and have their chips extracted. Milan pulls out her pocketknife and a few alcohol pads to prepare for the procedure.

Both David and Paris lunge forward reacting to Milan's abrasiveness.

"No, Milan! It's too deep they must be surgically removed, or at least under local anesthesia."

David and his colleagues were adamant about keeping the girls separate so they would be harder to capture. Each family lives in a different part of the Country and they keep communication minimal.

Milan asks about the artifacts they need to find and their importance. David clearly had no intention of sharing specific details about what had been hidden. He lets the ladies know that they must find the locations before Legion does and they'll know what lies beneath when it's been uncovered. There is a catch to the hunt. The coordinates hidden on the microchips are in the form of a riddle and only provide a broad area of location. In order to pinpoint the exact location, the ladies must solve the riddle. The locations will be hard to find but hidden in plain sight.

Milan and Paris aren't too fond of the idea of going on a scavenger hunt and now that Paris is safe Milan is ready to get back to work to sort through her coworkers and weed out the dirty officers.

"Milan there is no going back, this is the new normal. Don't you know you're being hunted. You and Paris. You can't go back, you'll be killed. You and Paris go find Lille and Marseille and have your chips extracted. Now that Legion knows you're a fighter they will come in full force. They will not rest until they get the information they are seeking."

"What information are they seeking. Don't beat around the bush David, just be completely honest with me."

Milan folds her arms and is visible disappointed with her father for keeping her out of the loop all these years and not trusting her with the truth.

"David? David is for everyone but you. I'm Dad to you."

David is also disappointed in himself for not sharing more. Milan could have been better prepared for both attacks had she known they were coming. David comes clean and shares that he had multiple army recruiters approach Milan to encourage her to join the military. He knew that she would get the combat training she needed to survive. Milan rolls her eyes at her father as she swiveled around in her chair to face the window.

"If it wasn't for the training, you would not have survived, Milan!"

"I nearly died twice because of what I didn't know, David! I admired you; I would have gladly followed your lead. No deception needed."

David is apologetic and assures Milan he made the best decision known to him.

David pulls out a burner phone and places it on the table in front of Milan. He instructs Milan and Paris to call Lille and Marseille and to set an appointment to have their chips extracted on the same day. The ladies' telephone numbers as well as the number to David's personal surgeon have been stored in the phone. David pulls out a briefcase from under the table and places it on top. He opens the black briefcase revealing stacks of cash filled to the brim. Milan and Paris lean back in their seats, creating distance between them and the money as if it is somehow tainted. David pushes the money closer to their side of the table when they lean back.

"This will get you where you need to go. You will be traveling to multiple countries throughout Europe, and you will need to use cash wherever you go."

David pulls an envelope from a compartment on the roof of the briefcase. He pulls out passports and identification cards for all four of the ladies. Milan and Paris find the I.D. cards with their photos and pseudonyms in place of their names. David tells the ladies to follow him as he walks out of the room. They walk to the back of the house and to a dwelling smaller than the home that resembles a barn. David leads them to a black jeep inside the massive space and hands Milan the keys.

"It's completely bulletproofed and buoyant. It was designed to withstand military grade attacks and keep you alive as long as possible but, use wisdom, it's not indestructible."

Milan and Paris enter the truck and set up the GPS to locate the closest of the two ladies, which happens to be Lille. David stands in the driveway as Paris reverses out. Milan and David lock eyes before they pull off. They are aware of the possibility that this may be the last time they see the other alive, so they sit in the moment for a while before Milan exits the vehicle, leaving the door open and runs over to David. They embrace and hold one another tight just in case this is the last time.

"I forgive you for everything, and everything will be ok."

Milan says through her shaking voice. David tries to mask his emotion as tears well in his eyes. As David's tears drip on Milan's shoulder, she rests his head on her shoulder and wraps her arms around his neck. Milan had never witnessed deep emotion from her father. She felt honored that he felt safe enough to express them to her. She pulls his shirt from the hem and uses it to dry his tears. They both chuckle as she wipes his face before exchanging "I love you's". Milan walks back to the jeep and she and Paris pull off.

Lille lives two states away from David's place, about a half a day's drive. Milan mounts the burner phone to a clip attached to the air vent. She calls Lille to formally introduce herself and Paris before they arrive at her home. Lille doesn't answer and they proceed on their journey. Six hours later they reach their destination according to the GPS coordinates. They stop at a path along a dirt road. The path is surrounded by trees and resembles a forest until they turn onto the path and drive a few yards in. They travel beyond the wooded area and pass a dead-end sign. They stumble upon a place they know can only be found if you know what you are looking for or run into if you're lost. The small cul-de-sac has been strategically hidden from view and is not welcome to outsiders. An upscale neighborhood is revealed, with large modern glass homes with luxury cars in the driveways and well-manicured lawns. Paris perks up in her seat as they get closer to Lille's home.

They receive a text message as they approach the charcoal grey home.

"Pull into the driveway, up to the ball trees."

Milan pulls into the driveway and stops at two potted trees, one on each side. They were not prepared for the concrete to separate and the jeep to descend into the lower parts of the home. Milan and Paris are startled by the jolt and sudden movement into the ground. They both grab their door handles and contemplate making a run for it. Milan quickly activates the location feature on the phone just in case. They are surrounded by concrete on all sides as they continue to descend to what feels like has no end. The jeep stops abruptly facing a room constructed of black reflective glass on all sides. A young woman wearing biker shorts and a sports bra emerges from a stairway on the opposite end of the garage sized room. The woman is short and extremely fit. She waves hello to Milan and Paris and motions for them to pull into the room. Milan pulls up behind a black Maserati sports car.

The woman pushes a button on the wall and the light fades as the car lift ascends back into the driveway. Milan places her pistol on her waist on the back of her pants and she Paris exits the vehicle with apprehension. As a trained fighter, Milan is always mindful of the exit points in every room she enters. They are completely enclosed and have no idea what awaits beyond the room they are sitting in. Milan doesn't know how familiar her father is with the women she and Paris have been charged to find but, he is known to leave out plenty of important detail. The woman cheerfully approaches Milan and Paris as she places her cup of tea in her left hand to extend the other for Milan to shake.

"Marseille. You must be Milan."

The woman says with an air of duplicity as she locks eyes with Milan. Milan's instincts tell her Marseille is hiding something but plays coy. Marseille greets Paris by name and invites the women to join her upstairs. Paris and Milan glance at one another with shared suspicion and follow Marseille since they have no other option at the moment.

They reach the top of the shiny black glass stairs and enter a dining area. A dark-haired slender woman sits at a thick glass communal dining room table with a smile as she stands to greet the ladies. She introduces herself as Lille and invites Milan and Paris to sit at the table. The table is covered with photos, letters, and documents new and old.

"I know you're probably wondering why we were all named after cities in France, except for you, Milan."

It is apparent Lille is the oldest in the group and seems to be privy to information the rest have been left in the dark about. Milan looks at Lille and waits for her to divulge more information before she speaks.

"Did David tell you who you are?"

"Who I am?"

Milan is confused but prepares herself for the full truth if Lille gives it up.

"Did he tell you why your father named you Milan?"

"Why my father named me Milan? Why would you say it that way?

Milan is confused and growing agitated. She removes her jacket and demands Lille to tell her what she knows. Lille places a photo in front of Milan. The man in the photo is wearing a military uniform and has reddish brown hair. The photo is dated for the year 1999, four years after Milan was born.

"From what my father tells me your father was a great man. My dad was heartbroken when he found out he was killed."

Lille shares with genuine empathy while pulling additional photos to share with the ladies. She places three photos alongside the mysterious man's photo. Milan stares blankly as she looks down at the photo and back at Lille.

"Who is this man? I've never seen him before, in my life."

"Milan, that's your father Joseph. He died when you were four and your God parents adopted you and raised you as their own. I figured they told you about your father. I didn't mean to shock you, we thought you knew."

Lille shares with concern as she shares a photo of a man and woman unfamiliar to Milan. Milan has risen from the table without any further acknowledgment of the information. She puts on her jacket and prepares to leave.

"They are your godparents David and Gloria."

Paris picks up the photo and takes a closer look.

"That's not David. We just left David, that's definitely not him."

Paris hands the photo to Milan.

"I don't know what types of games you two are playing but we've got bigger fish to fry. These chips need to be removed within 24 hours and the information needs to be extracted before we can move any further."

Lille and Marseille look at one another and shrug.

"I can assure you there are no games being played here, I just thought you may want the photos as keepsakes. My father dug them up for you because he knew you didn't have much interaction with your father before he died but, if it's too overwhelming we can move on."

Marseille says in a snarky tone.

Milan rejoins the women at the table and Lille pulls out her tablet. She has the profiles of Legion's leaders and the coordinates of their next few moves. This will give them an idea of how much time they have to move undetected before going overseas. Lille pulls up a photo grid of some of the people tied to legion. Both Paris and Milan recognized members of the group. A few of Milan's fellow police officers, the men that followed and abducted her as well as the man who held Paris captive were among the group. Lille swipes on her screen a few times before revealing the ringleader of the terrorist group.

"This is the one we need to look out for. He is ruthless and will kill without merci. They call him The Grand Hydra. Kill him and two more twice as vicious will emerge from the shadows. That's why they've been after us four, to find all ties to him and cut the problem off completely at the root."

Milan and Paris both scream and jump back in their seats when Lille shows them a photo of David as the ringleader of Legion.

"No, that's David my father!"

Milan proclaims. Lille and Marseille are startled by the screams, and they also jump back into their seats.

"Where is this information coming from? They have been after my father for years! Who is your source?!"

"My father, the one who witnessed David murder your father after having him ambushed on the battlefield. They called it friendly fire."

Marseille says. Her elbows are resting on her knees, her hands are laced together, and her look is piercing. Marseille couldn't wait to share the news with Milan, she was delighted in fact.

Paris grabs Milan's arm and shares a look of pity.

"This can't be right! I will get to the bottom of this. It must be a set up."

Milan is on her feet pacing back and forth at the table. Milan looks at Paris and lets her know she is going to talk to David face to face. Paris gets up without hesitation to join Milan.

"We'll go with you; we can take my car."

Lille says as she gets up and grabs her keys. Milan looks down the stairs to the lower level and back at Lille and Marseille. Her gut is telling her to take her own vehicle and ditch the two ladies. However, she wants the freedom to maneuver on her phone and do some digging before reaching David. Milan decides to take Lille up on her offer to drive them to David's. Milan looks at Paris and can see distrust in her eyes. They are both ignoring the warning signals and acting in haste. They have shared sentiment, but they proceed anyway. Milan and Paris follow the women to a stand-alone garage in the back of the house. They pile into a large black jeep, Lille in the driver's seat, Marseille in the passenger seat and Milan and Paris in the back. Lille backs the jeep out of the garage, and they drive up a hill in the opposite direction away from the main road.

Both Paris and Milan look down when Milan's phone vibrates. David's name pops up on the caller I.D. with a request for a video call. Paris stares at the phone screen blankly, waiting to see what Milan will do next. Milan hesitates then decides there is no time like the present to confront David. She answers and puts the phone on speaker. David and two women are on the screen, one on either side.

"Hey, Milan. The ladies are already here. You probably made it at least halfway to Lille's place already, but you all have been compromised. You may need to lay low before turning back."

Lille and Marseille glance at one another sharing looks of malice while Milan and Paris are frozen in place. David observes the looks of fear plastered on the faces of Milan and Paris and regrets oversharing before ensuring that the coast was clear.

"Who's driving?" David asks, worried.

Just then, the car veers off the main road and Lille and Marseille jump out of the vehicle while it's still in motion. The jeep plunges into a steep stretch of trees leading to a ravine as Marseille and Lille dive into a cluster of hedges before the steep drop. Milan and Paris brace themselves for impact. Milan drops her phone, they put on their seatbelts then shield their heads with their arms. They pull their heads down to their laps and lean into the seats in front of them to hopefully, minimize injury upon impact. The sound of David's voice shouting from the phone fills the air as the phone slides under the driver's seat.

Milan starts to pray.

"Lord please forgive me for my sins and deliver Paris and I from a premature death, please! In Jesus' name."

Paris looks at Milan with confusion. She never struck Milan to be a religious person. She never even heard her mention God in all the time they spent together.

Milan's life begins to flash before her eyes. She is suddenly aware that this moment has been known to precede death. She has a vision of herself as a toddler sharing special moments with her parents. Then a flash of a baby that she had never met in a basinet. The vision of the baby is inversed, and she can see from the baby's perspective. She is watching her parents David and Pearl smiling at her looking into her basinet. The vision is quick and lasts for seconds before the jeep smashes into a tree. The impact causes the jeep to split in two from the back with Milan and Paris on either side of the split.

Chapter 4

Upheaval

Day turns to night when Paris regains consciousness. She is alarmed by the darkness surrounding her. She is hopeful when she catches the reflection of the moon dancing on the stream at the bottom of the ravine. She tries to push her side door open, but the hinges of the door have impaled the tree the jeep is now merged with. The cool breeze flowing through the vehicle from her left prompts her to feel around for an opening. As she reaches out, she nearly falls through the split and onto the dirt. The moonlight shines in and on the side of Milan's face. She is leaning on the door and is not moving. Her head rests in the groove of cracked glass from the impact and her blood is dispersed around the crack. Paris quickly checks Milan's pulse, which is faint, but she is breathing. In a panic Paris yanks her seatbelt aggressively trying to release the jam. Instead, she slides her slender frame up and out of confinement. Standing in between the split leaning into the jeep, Paris checks Milan's pockets for the keys to her jeep back at the house. She retrieves them from Milan's pocket and feels around the floor of

51

the vehicle for her cell phone. After searching for a few moments, she finds it on the driver's side floor.

Paris uses the light from the moon to navigate the dark wooded area. As she walked away from the scene Paris soon realized the only tree standing tall enough to catch the jeep was the only reason, they had not flown into the steep ravine below. Walking away from the accident with minimal injury enabled Paris to trek up the hill with ease. Paris carefully steps on the roots protruding from nearby trees to climb the grassy hill leading to the road ahead. Paris reaches the road; solar powered streetlamps light the way. She looks back at her path below and studies the opening so she can retrace her steps. Across the road is a small brown colored barn at the center of a small stretch of land. Paris scurries across the road and is conscious of the volume of the sound of her footsteps as she searches for Lille's home.

Ten minutes into her walk she spots Lille's driveway, on her right. She crouches down close to the ground and runs across the back of the property behind the home. Flood lights near the double garage doors illuminate the path leading to the back of the house. Aside from the floodlights the black siding on the home makes it nearly impossible to see. A door on the side of the home swings open. Paris stands up against a neighboring fence. A portion of the fence is shielded by a dark shadow. With seconds to decide, Paris stands in the shadow and can only hope she is completely hidden from view. The two women who ditched the jeep and tried to kill her and Milan emerge from the home. The woman posing as Marseille lights a cigarette as the other walks with her to the back yard of the home. Paris carefully tiptoes toward the door which they left ajar. Paris is unable to breathe until she finally reaches the door as the women's backs are turned. She makes her way into the basement door which is only a few feet away from the back entrance.

The stairway down to the basement is pitch black along with the black painted walls. With little time to get out of the home, Paris walks down the stairs with her arms extended to the walls on either side of the stairs. Paris stops when her hand glides onto a large protrusion on the wall. She presses into it, and it inserts into the wall. The room is resonating with the echoing reverberations of a significant shift. She is three steps away from the bottom of the stairs and it is still dark. Paris continues until she touches a switch a few inches from the button. The lights flicker on, and Milan's jeep is where she left it. The driveway lift has descended so, Paris quickly jumps int the jeep and backs it into the lift. She sits in the jeep and panics when she is unable to determine how to operate the lift to ascend. She exits the vehicle and feels around the walls of the stone covered lift. Paris locates a switch on the wall behind the jeep. She lets out a sigh of relief when the lift starts to move. She hops back in and counts the seconds until the lift comes to a complete stop on the ground level.

Paris looks around the area in a panic as the jeep reaches the driveway. The sun peers through the hills on the horizon beyond the dense forest outside of the secluded patch of homes. Paris has lost track of time and can assume she and Milan have been unconscious and left for dead for most of the night. As she backs out of the driveway, she stops abruptly to avoid crashing into one of the three additional trucks blocking the entrance to the driveway. Paris quickly swerves around the vehicles and drives across the lawn. The windows on the jeeps are completely tinted so Paris is not aware if she was spotted but she speeds up the road to the crash site and does not look back.

Paris parks in front of the opening and rushes down to the crash site in search of Milan. When she reaches the jeep Milan is gone. She frantically searches the area and spots a set of footsteps leading away from the jeep. Milan is lying on the ground on her stomach a few yards away. Milan's eyes are wide open, and she is completely still. Paris kneels closer to Milan's body and rests her head on her back. The sound of gurgled breathing provides some hope. Milan blinks her eyes and offers a slight smile.

Without hesitation Paris puts one of Milan's arms around her neck and pulls her up. Milan lays her wounded head on Paris and limps with Paris to the jeep. She helps Milan into the passenger seat and gives her a towel from the backseat to rest her head on and cover her wound.

"Milan you should probably stay awake since you hit your head pretty hard. You may not wake up if you don't."

Milan's eyes widen and she perks up in her seat following Paris' precautions. Paris speeds down the road and out of the secluded neighborhood. They don't even look at the house nor do they look back until they make it to the main road a few miles away.

Milan remembers the distress in David's voice yelling through the phone before she blacked out. She pulls her phone charger from the glove box and charges her cell phone. Once there is enough battery power to turn the phone back on dozens of notifications from missed calls and voicemail messages pop up on the screen. Milan proceeds to call her father when her mind is flooded with the images shown by the women at Lille's home. She doesn't know who to trust so she must find out what she can on her own before addressing David. She wants to call her mother, but she tells David every detail of Milan's life which may pose a danger now that his true identity may have been revealed.

Milan decides to take a chance and call her mother without causing alarm. She tells Pearl that she was on a road trip and was taking the scenic route. She asks her mother, Pearl, if she heard from David because she couldn't get a hold of him. Pearl tells Milan that she does not reach out to David, he calls her when he is

good and ready. Milan remains quiet for a few
moments to leave room for Pearl to divulge anything
voluntarily. After a while, Pearl stops talking and they
are both silent.

"Nothing is what it seems Milan. You father is a
good man and anything he has done for you was with
pure intentions. His distance over the years was for
our protection."

Pearl says followed by "talk to you soon." Before
hanging up the phone. Milan remained silent for the
duration of their conversation until the end.

A few hours into their drive Milan and Paris stop at
a motel to rest. They were able to pay in cash and a
little extra to avoid showing identification. The motel
shares a parking lot with a convenience store and a
small diner, so Milan was able to get supplies to treat
her wound temporarily before seeing a doctor. Once
they shower and change, they are relieved to finally sit
down and eat their first meal in over twenty-four
hours. They shovel their food and beverages down in
silence and take extra meals and drinks for the road.
Worried they will fall asleep and be tracked down,
they gather their belongings and checkout shortly after
they return to their rooms.

Paris drives for the remainder of the trip. They
reach David's home just before sundown and
immediately feel a shift in the atmosphere. Paris and

Milan stay in the jeep for a bit to surveille the area. No one is around and the stillness in the air is eerie. Neither of them speaks a word but shared concern is expressed through eye contact. Milan reaches into the backseat and grabs her pistol. She makes sure it's loaded before exiting the vehicle. Paris follows and they close their doors gently and walk toward the back of the house. They walk along the side of the home and look through the window peering into the living area and part of the kitchen.

Paris grabs Milan's arm firmly with terror in her eyes. Milan follows her line of sight leading to David lying in a pool of blood near the descending stairs in his living area. They rush around to the front of the house. Both of their hearts are racing, and they are riddled with fear. The front door is slightly open, and the locks and doorknob have been shot off. Paris stands on one side of the doorway while Milan leads with her pistol and slowly steps in. David moves his arm and attempts to grab his wound, a gunshot to his abdomen. Milan runs to David, removes her jacket, and presses it into his wound to stop the blood. Blood gushes from his back as she applies pressure, and he moans in agony. She tells Paris to hold the jacket in place while she searches for a towel to stop the blood.

Within seconds Milan glides across the floor and to David's side with towels for his wound.

"David! Who did this to you? Who was in the house?!"

"Legion."

David whispers.

"They're still here."

David points down and Milan looks down the stairs leading to the lower level. David is losing a lot of blood and is very weak. He grabs Milan's arm and pulls her close.

"They need your blood. It's extremely rare, remember that and believe nothing they tell you and half of what you see."

Milan brings her ear close to David's mouth so she can grasp every word. David releases his last breath, and his body goes limp.

Milan lays her head on David's chest to check for a heartbeat and his airway for beathing. There is no sign of life. Milan shakes him frantically while calling his name and starts performing chest compressions. After a few rounds of CPR, she checks his pulse and breath. All the pressure pushed onto David's body causes the release of more blood. In mid compression Paris gently touches Milan's shoulder and offers her condolences. The touch from Paris brings Milan back to reality.

David is gone and there isn't a doctor in town, in the middle of nowhere, that can help.

Milan remembers David gave her his surgeon's information before she left to meet Lille and Marseille. Milan paces the living area as she speaks with the doctor about David's condition. She completely forgot about what lies beneath in the lower level until a moving shadow is spotted from her peripheral vision as she stands near the stairs. She freezes in place and alerts Paris of movement on the lower level using hand gestures.

Milan draws her weapon, places her cell phone on the floor with the doctor still on the line and proceeds down the stairs. Paris walks behind Milan. They remain close to the right side of the stairs to stay out of sight as they approach the unknown.

Shots ring out outside the home as bullets ricochet off the glass exterior of the home. Paris and Milan duck and cover their heads. Once they determine the shots are being fired from outside, they move quickly down the stairs. Two women are bound with rope to chairs at the center of the room. The women are gagged, bare foot and blood is dripping from their big toes. Milan and Paris look at one another and immediately rush over to free the ladies. They know instantly who they are due to the evident search for the microchips in their toes. When the cloths covering their mouths are removed Milan remembers their faces from the video calls with her father.

"They're coming back for the chips. They couldn't find ours, but they will be back for yours."

One of the women says distressed yet relieved to see Milan and Paris.

Milan stoops down to get a closer look at the woman talking.

"There are two women at your home impersonating you. Who are you?" Milan asks.

"My name is Lille and this is Marseille. We all met as children at one of your mother's recitals."

Milan stands as she gets a flashback of being in the room, they're in. As Lille is speaking Milan walks to the back wall and feels around applying pressure simultaneously. After about a minute a loud click quiets the room, and a door opens. The other ladies rush over and stand in the doorway. Milan's third step inside the room triggers the lighting. A short corridor lies ahead with a path leading left at the end of it. The entire left side of the wall is a collection of guns big and small, artfully arranged by fire power. The firearms are behind a series of glass shields. Milan sticks her fingers through a slit in the glass casing and slides a portion of the glass open. A loud breaking sound snaps the ladies out of their shock, and they all look up toward the ceiling. A loud thud sound followed by loud footsteps send the women into a panic. They all rush to attempt to close the door before they are discovered. They pull the door closed until they hear a click. They instinctively start grabbing as many firearms and ammunition as they can carry, stuffing guns in their pants, their socks and in their bra straps. They have no choice but to follow the path they are on and hope it leads outside of the home. They turn the corner, and the path illuminates as they walk through. They walk twenty-five yards to stairs leading up to a door on the ceiling.

Milan slides tree latch locks and carefully opens the door. She looks around before stepping all the way through the doorway. They are amazed to find themselves in David's garage. Milan never noticed the trapdoor during her time spent with David inside the garage because it seamlessly blends into the grey cement colored floor. There are two vehicles in front of them, a black sports car, and a black jeep. Milan frantically searches for keys to either vehicle when she remembers David's warning about Legion being in his home.

"Who had you two tied up in the basement?"

"We blacked out after being hit in the back of our heads. We woke up tied up and bloody."

Lille says.

"Who or what did you see?"

"No one after we blacked out. The last person we saw was David."

Milan and Paris look at one another with wide eyes.

"I heard people talking and they were aware that you and Paris were at my family home. They said you were already dead. They were planning to take the chips, bring your bodies here and torch the home with all of us in it."

Milan skates over Marseille's story. She doesn't know who to trust, including her father's word.

"We exchanged text messages when I got to your house."

Milan says suspiciously.

"They must have found a way to intercept my calls. I've been here with Marseille and your father. We decided to come and meet you here because our fathers were worried, we had somehow been compromised." Lille shares.

Suddenly, the double garage doors open. Everyone looks around to see who found the garage door opener. Everyone shares in the confusion. When the doors ascend two women and a few men wearing black suits and dark shades stand in front of three SUV's and watches them intently until the door opens completely.

Chapter 5

Logan

A woman approaches Milan and offers condolences for the loss of her father.

"We'll handle Legion and David's body until you and your family are ready to prepare for funeral services."

The woman says sincerely.

Paris, Marseille, and Lille gather around Milan to hear what the woman is saying.

"Who are you?" Milan asks.

"Agent Logan, I work with your father. I don't know how much he has shared with you but when he was shot, he sent out an alert for you ladies. We need to get you to the surgeon immediately."

Agent Logan follows the trail of blood on the ground to Marseille and Lille.

"We'll someone tend to the wounds on your feet on the way. Load up and we'll talk more on the way."

The ladies follow Logan to one of the jeeps.

"Milan, take the front seat." Logan says.

They enter the large three-row SUV. The back of the jeep is open, and the last row has been converted to a two-passenger row facing the back window with small benches on either side. Marseille and Lille are instructed to enter through the back. A woman wearing a black suit and white sterile gloves follows and shuts the door behind them. Paris sits behind logan.

As they pull out of the driveway a black truck similar in appearance to a coroner's vehicle sits in front with a man wearing a white lab coat in the driver's seat. He writes on a clipboard as another man gets in on the passenger 's side. Milan hangs her head in grief as they pass by the truck. They ride through David's property off the usual path leading to the main road. Logan drives around the garage and onto a dirt path through the wooded area behind the home. Milan and Paris perk up and observe as they ride through a compound. A patch of upscale cabin style homes with about an acre of land in between them. The homes look new and empty.

Logan looks at Milan for any familiarity in her facial expression. Milan is surprised to see this side of the land; one she hadn't seen before. Logan slows down to a complete stop.

"David was building this for you. You, your mother, David's mother, and his brother. He was planning to retire and invite you all to come and stay on his property. Each of you with your own home for you and your families to live comfortably. This is yours now."

Milan looks away and holds back tears of conviction. She was effectively convinced her father was the villain, someone that would do all but protect her despite his efforts since her youth. The secrets her father carried only fueled the rumors and reinforced the efficacy of Legion's plan to cause confusion and untimely death for the ladies.

Agent Logan drives along a path traveling around the newly discovered Brown family compound. The dirt path leads through a forest surrounded by thick evergreen trees with large rocks and mountains peering through in the distance. They stop in front of a large black gate leading to a road overlooking the seacoast. Logan places her thumb print over an app on her phone and the dual swing gate opens inward. They drive along the coast for a few miles until they reach a massive white structure reminiscent of a concentric castle. The ocean expands beyond the massive landscape and the road ahead leads into the sun's rays as it touches the horizon as it sets.

The outer wall extends well above the trees and expands across most of the land. Beyond the fortress lies a network of buildings within. They turn onto the property and into a wide path descending into the lower part of the property. The fine architecture is a combination of medieval and modern, well maintained, and sterile looking. When they reach the bottom of the driveway a strong, bald man emerges from a walkway parallel to the driveway. He approaches the vehicle and looks at Logan intently. No words were exchanged during the stare down. The strong man nods at Logan and she nods back then the stone wall before them slides open and they drive in. Once inside the dimly lit empty space they drive onto an elevator lift with two sets of doors. The metal doors close, and a computer screen emerges from the side of the doors. Logan pulls her dark shades up and a blue light shines bright and scans her eyes. The lift ascends and everyone is silent during the ride. Milan looks back at Paris, who shares a look of worry.

The Lift stops and the door opens to the blue sky. They ride around a bend to an overpass leading to the inner court of the property. The overpass extends through two of the buildings with elevator access to each building. They reach the last building on the bridge and turn left into an open parking garage. Logan parks near an elevator. They walk toward the stainless-steel door and logan presses a few buttons on her watch before scanning it on a touch pad on the wall. The door opens and everyone follows Logan inside. The elevator moves forward for a couple of seconds before briefly descending. They reach an executive suite with stark white walls and a spotless burgundy carpet. Logan leads the group to the right and to a set of double doors. The censored doors slide open as they approach. The doors open to a wall with a metal staircase on either side. The stairs on the left lead to the mechanical system of the building. Without a second thought Logan walks down the stairs to the right. At the center of the sterile, white room is a large cubical curtain suspended from the ceiling.

The four ladies stand in awe of the space as Logan and the medic that rode with them pull the medical curtains open around a circular rod revealing four hospital beds. The beds are positioned in a half circle with a medical cart equipped with sterile tools, next to each bed. An older man wearing surgical scrubs emerges with a steel cart on wheels.

"Hello ladies. You've been long awaited."

He says warmly as he pushes the cart in front of the beds.

"Please, pick your bed and take a seat. Let's get started."

Milan, Paris, Lille and Marseille each choose a bed and sit upright.

"They call me The Doctor. You ladies may already know what your fathers do for a living. We all work for Special Forces in the U.S. military. We work directly for the government. Or at least we did, but that's another story for another day."

Paris and Milan glance at one another with concern. Lille and Marseille continue to sit and listen unphased. The doctor catches the exchange between Milan and Paris and directs his attention to them.

"You must be David's daughter, Milan, right?"

Milan responds with a "yes".

"Not to worry your father is in good hands."

The doctor says and winks at Milan. Milan is unsure how to take the message but assumes the doctor is referring to the preparation of his body before his memorial service. The doctor sets up his tools for the extraction when he takes notice of the bandages on Lille and Marseille's feet.

"Oh, no they found your chips."

The doctor says with mild concern.

Lille removes her nose ring and Marseille, one of her earrings. They disassemble the backings from their studs revealing the gold, square shaped microchips. They hold their microchips in their hands and extend their arms with pride as they showcase the evidence of outsmarting their captors.

There was an attempt to abduct Lille and Marseille when they were teenagers. After the traumatizing ordeal they had their chips removed and hidden in their jewelry. They never removed the jewelry until today. They were told to tell no one about the chips until the doctor was prepared to extract them.

"Very well done."

The doctor says as he approaches them with a petri dish. The ladies are instructed to place the chips in the dish and the doctor sets them on his steel cart.

A woman dressed in surgical scrubs joins the doctor and preps Paris and Milan for their extractions. They begin with Milan. She is instructed to lay down on her back and her toe is wiped with an iodine solution to disinfect her skin. A small green surgical drape is placed around her toe and the doctor injects her with a local anesthetic. After a couple of minutes, he uses a scalpel and makes a small incision in her toe. The doctor uses medical tweezers to remove the chip. Milan gags at the sight of the doctor burrowing inside her toe for the chip, so she looks away until the extraction is complete. He places the specimen on the petri dish and stiches Milan's wound closed. The doctor proceeds with Paris's extraction and hands the filled dish to his assistant.

The doctor preps Milan's arm for blood extraction. He fills two tubes with her blood and hands her one.

"You'll know what to do with this when the time comes."

Milan is confused but she complies and puts the blood flow tube in her pocket.

The medical assistant covers Milan and Paris' feet with bandages, a sock and provides all four ladies with post-surgery open toe shoes for their travels.

"Why don't you ladies go down to the canteen for a meal. Today's special is Croque Monsieur. We should have the info you need by the time you return."

The doctor says with exceptional delight.

Logan leads the ladies to the canteen on the lower level. The four ladies hadn't eaten all day and helped themselves to multiple servings of the buffet style meals. The unpredictable events that have transpired over the past few days has forced the women into a state of survival. They each pack an additional protein packed meal, fruit, and beverages to go.

When they get back to the room the doctor and his assistant are waiting in front of a projector and computer. Four chairs are reserved for the women facing the projector screen.

"Agent Logan, I'm afraid the women must go at it alone from this point forward. They have a life altering mission ahead and the blueprint is for them alone."

Without hesitation Logan hands Milan a cell phone and tells her to "call anytime if she or any of the ladies need anything." Milan accepts the phone and is noticeably confused and concerned. "I won't ever be too far behind. I promised your father." Logan's words provide some ease for Milan. She has the most combat and survival training among the ladies and feels responsible for everyone.

The doctor has extracted the information from the chips. He enlarges a composite photo created with an image from each chip. The ladies sit up in their seats and lean forward to get a closer look at the photo. A map of Europe with location points on four major cities; Paris France, Lille France, Marseille France, and Milan Italy.

The doctor tells the ladies there is something important hidden in each city. Something that they need to find. The women must travel to Europe, each to their namesake city and uncover the specific location.

"To find what, exactly?"

Marseille says, hardly interested in a scavenger hunt.

"I'll print all the coordinates for you ladies but, there are some things you must discover on your own. There are codes that must be cracked and puzzles that must be pieced together. I cannot do it for you, you four must do it together."

The women stare at the doctor in silence. They are exhausted from their recent ordeals with Legion and Milan and Paris are unsure who they can trust.

"And if we don't? What's at stake?"

Milan asks.

"Humanity. Life as we know it will be at stake. All that your fathers sacrificed and risked their lives to protect will all be in vain."

Milan turns back and looks at the open doorway behind them.

"You are free to go. No one will stop you; you have free will but when everything rises to the surface you will wish you had followed through, and you will live to regret it."

Milan stands, gathers her belongings, and walks toward the door. The remainder of the women remain seated and wait to hear more from the doctor. The doctor speaks in an elevated tone of voice so Milan can hear him clearly as she leaves the room.

"There is a reason you are being sent to the cities you were named for. This mission has been in the works since before you four were even born. You were made for such a time as this."

Milan stops in her tracks but doesn't turn around as the doctor is speaking. The memory of David and his plans to bring the family to live together flashes in Milan's mind. She may never know David's true identity nor his intentions if she doesn't jump down the rabbit hole for the truth. Everyone sits quietly and watches Milan to see what she will do next. Milan turns back and joins the group to uncover the content on the chips.

"Ok, show me everything." Milan rests her belongings on the floor and perks up in her seat ready to uncover the truth.

"Now that's the spirit."

The doctor says with glee.

The doctor prints all the information from the microchips. Sending them electronically would pose a security risk. Each of the women receive their own stack of coordinates with a detailed photo of a map of their designated city on top of the stack. The ladies are instructed to travel to their designated cities separately until each mission is complete.

"What are we looking for?"

Paris asks the doctor.

"All the information you need is on the paperwork. You'll have to sort through it and figure it out."

The doctor and his assistant pushed the cart and all the medical gear out of the room and shut the door behind them. Milan places her stack on the floor and spreads the sheets of paper out before her. She gets on her knees and the rest of the women follow her lead. Below Milan's map is a sheet of paper with a gold square in the upper left corner and a passage in small font beside the shape. Milan reads the passage out loud.

"A bridge in the Alps over the Simplon Pass, a road to Paris through Jupiter's Gate. When Roman walls fall Cagnola will rise triumphant, to find a place for Castelprio's fate."

"Huh"

They all say in unison.

"I don't think we have time for riddles, but it looks like I've got one too, with a gold shape on the sheet."

Paris holds up her sheet of paper with the corner of a gold square in the top right corner of the sheet. She reads hers aloud as well.

"A seat at the opera, twenty to be precise, to defend the Arche dessous Triumphal Way."

Both Lille and Marseille search their stacks for a similar sheet. They place their sheets on the floor, with both papers connected creating half of a square on the bottom. Milan and Paris place their sheets below Lille and Marseille's creating a perfect square. Each riddle serves as a guide to the discovery of whatever is hidden that they are being forced to uncover. The gold square is the key and will guide them to the exact point of entry. They will find what is hidden only if instructions are followed to the "T" and the riddle is solved correctly.

Milan, Paris, Marseille, and Lille spend hours studying the information, going over each page with a fine-tooth comb. They learn more about their fathers during this time of discovery than throughout their lives.

"The Porte de L'orient at the Marseille Easter Gate. My father brought me here when I was little."

Marseille holds up a sheet of paper with a photo of her and her father near a statue in front of a body of water. The rest of the ladies move in closer to investigate.

"My father told me I would be back here one day; it was my destiny."

Marseille adds.

"What else do you remember while you were there? Milan asks.

"My dad left me in the hotel room for half the day one day. I don't know what he was doing all that time but, I know he wanted me to be familiar with the water. Swimming and diving lessons were mandatory up until I went away for college. During this trip we memorized the different monuments and buildings near the shore. Marseille hurriedly grabs her sheet and reads the passage.

"Heroes and victims of the sea, below the gate there were three."

"I was named for this place. We were all named for the cities we are assigned to, and we need to figure out why. What happened during the time of our births that encouraged our connections to these places."

Marseille continues.

The ladies look at one another and share concern. A life-changing secret has been kept from them their entire lives, but it encompasses their very existence. None of them knew the other personally before a last week but they realize they will be bonded for life through this adventure. Their fathers purposely kept them separate because of the microchips. When the attempted abductions began, they didn't want to make it easy or Legion to get a hold of all the ladies at once. It is imperative that the women travel to each city destination alone, for this reason.

"We must dig into the fathers' past to figure that out. What were they involved in when they forged a connection? Did we inherit a problem or a blessing? I would like to figure this out and be done with this already, I have no interest in a scavenger hunt for international treasure."

Paris says with irritation in her voice.

Milan hangs her head as she is reminded of her recent loss. She is overcome by grief. She feels as though the walls are caving in on her and her air supply is dissipating.

"I have to bury my father first. I can't even think about any of this now."

Milan gets up from the floor and leaves the room to get some fresh air. She steps outside and finds an overpass overlooking the main courtyard. She rests her arms on the white stucco ledge and rests her head in her hands. The cool breeze from Evening air improves her breathing and calms her rattled nerves. Movement from a neighboring building in the courtyard catches Milan's eye. A woman wearing white is fluffing pillows and dressing a bed. The woman seems to be a maid or porter. Windows throughout the building reveal a similar layout, a bed, desk, and possible living quarters. Milan rejoins the women and tells them about her sighting. They are all exhausted from their tumultuous ordeals and are eager for a shower and some rest in a safe place. They gather their belongings and limp out of the room in hopes of gaining access to the neighboring building.

The ladies walk through a set of double doors leading to a skybridge to the building. They are unsure which way to turn so they travel a straight path until they see a woman pushing a cleaning cart. Milan tells the woman they need rooms to rest. The woman does not speak but, without hesitation gives the ladies four key cards to the rooms she just finished preparing. The ladies graciously accept and enter their rooms, four rooms neighboring one another. They plan to retreat for the night and regroup in the morning.

Chapter 6

David

A single white rose is offered to Milan and her mother as they enter the church for her father's funeral service. David's Parents and brother Daniel follow behind them. They are the first guests to arrive. Milan and her mother walk arm and arm through the small sanctuary. The side walls are lined with white roses and other floral bouquets. Two men wearing military uniforms stand at attention on either side of the casket. Milan releases her arm from her mother's grip and walks toward the black casket draped with the American flag. She glides her hand over the flag and inserts her rose into the cluster of white roses on top. Milan looks around subtly and discreetly lifts the corner of the casket revealing a white satin lining and No body!

Milan's eyes widen and she carefully closes the casket top. She rushes over to her mother and informs her about the empty casket.

"What do you mean it's empty?!" Pearl says, astonished.

Logan and a few others walk into the church and greet Milan and her family. Milan tries to maintain her composure as she tells Logan about her father's missing body. Logan pauses for a moment and tells Milan to "just relax, everything will be fine. I'm sure there is a logical explanation for this."   Logan approaches one of the soldiers near the casket but speaks loud enough for both to hear.

"Open the casket Seargeant." The soldier stands still and continues to look forward.

"I can't do that for you ma'am. Strict orders."

The other soldier looks at the casket, curiously but bridles his curiosity and looks forward.

"Orders from whom?"

Logan asks. The soldier doesn't answer. Logan motions for Milan to come over. Instinctively, Milan knew what to do. Without saying another word, they both remove the bouquet and the flag and grab a corner of the casket and open it. The soldiers stand still and do not interfere. Gasps fill the air from attendees as they pour into the room and spot the empty casket.

The two soldiers keep their focus on the doors at the front of the church and they calmly walk out in silence. David's mother grabs her chest in shock as Daniel comforts her. The Brown family looks to Milan for

answers. She has been known for cracking the
toughest cases including keeping track of her father,
surely, she can locate David once again.

Milan looks at Logan and waits for a response.
Logan doesn't seem surprised or bothered by the
discovery. Milan feels Logan wanted her to see the
empty casket. She seems to know more than she's
letting on.

"We need to go." Logan says to Milan.

You and the other daughters need to complete your
mission, I'll find David.

"Is he really dead, Logan."

Milan asks firmly.

"Whatever state he's in, I will find him. This may
just be a ruse to delay your connection to your assigned
locations. Remember, whatever you all have, there is a
network of people ready to hunt and kill for it. They
will not stop until they find you and stop you or you
stop them. You need to go, now!"

Logan says convincingly.

Milan leaves the church and goes back to her secret
apartment in the city. She hadn't been back since She
and Paris fled to David's home. She parks her car a
few blocks away and walks through a neighboring

alley to remain unnoticed. She eagerly walks toward her mailbox to retrieve a manila envelope protruding from her mailbox. She places her thumb print in her keypad and unlocks her front door. Milan draws her firearm and stands completely still and quiet to listen for any movement in her place. With her weapon drawn and pointed toward the floor she sweeps her place thoroughly for any monitoring bugs or signs of entry. Once she is confident her security has not been breached, Milan settles in her office and opens the envelope.

Inside the envelope is the deed to David's land including all the properties on the one-hundred-acre lot. Milan pulls a set of keys from the envelope, keys to all properties. She unfolds a thick poster sized paper and spreads the sheet across her desk, covering the entire surface. It is a map of sublevel tunnels and dwellings under the land. In true military fashion David burrowed through a large portion of his land digging out ditches for booby traps and built escape hatches below each dwelling that lead to the outer perimeters of the property line. He provided multiple avenues of escape and a clear plan of action in the event of an ambush.

Milan gathers some supplies from her home including a first aid kit, water, dry snacks and painkillers, a couple of firearms and ammunition. She packs all she can fit in a backpack and heads toward the door. Before she leaves, Milan checks the video feed on the cameras on the exterior of her property. The coast is clear, so she heads back to her car cutting through a different alley on a parallel street. She disarms her car alarm as she approaches and before she takes a step into the street, her car explodes. The impact knocks Milan off her feet and sends her body flying back into someone's garage door. The impact of her body slamming into the concrete was softened by her backpack on her back. People come out of their homes and buildings to witness and videorecord the event. Milan's hearing is muffled by ringing in her ears. A few people inch closer with their cell phones as they look for potential victims to capture on video. Milan moves quickly to avoid being captured on video. She crawls around the corner into an alley. The only person who she feels she can trust in this moment is Logan. She sends her a text message and asks her to pick her up due to an emergency. Milan can only hope Logan doesn't have any covert plans and is secretly working with Legion, but she doesn't have a choice she must trust her blindly.

Logan responds within a minute and asks Milan for her location. She tells her and warns her about the explosion and to meet her in the alley off the main road. Milan crawls along the path of garages and lifts each one in passing in hopes to find one unlocked. She reaches the middle of the alley and finds a garage door that has been left open. She uses the flashlight on her cell phone to look inside before lifting the door up completely. The garage is empty and there is a lockbox on the door leading to the inside of the home. Milan looks at the windows on the second level of the home, the curtains are drawn, and the place looks empty inside. Milan pushes her backpack inside and crawls into the garage and closes the door behind her. She leans up against the wall closest to the garage door and leans her head back on the wall. As soon as she feels some relief she thinks of Paris, Marseille and Lille and potential bomb threats against them. She sends a group text and checks on them.

The Ladies never left the secret headquarters and they have yet to uncover the secret or who the mysterious place is for. Whether it be FBI, CIA, Internal Affairs, the US Military, or all of the above, it remains a mystery. All information is provided on a need-to-know basis and questions were met with vague answers or evaded completely. Paris, Lille nor Marseille heard any news about attacks on their properties or families however, Marseille has yet to check on her family home since the Legion invasion. They all agree that staying put may have saved their lives.

Logan texts Milan and lets her know she has arrived and is in the alley. Milan opens the garage door slowly and while on her knees, she pokes her head out to check for Logan's jeep. When Milan turns her head to the left a jeep at the end of the alley flashes the headlights twice. Milan limps toward the jeep and gets in. Logan grabs a roll of paper towel from the back seat and hands it to Milan. Milan looks down confused until she pulls down the passenger side mirror and sees the blood dripping down from her ears. She rolls a few sheets around her hand and presses it into her ears.

"I'll take you back to the headquarters, you'll be safe there."

"I have to get a couple of things before we go.

"So, they can blow up your home next? Not a good idea. I promised David, I would keep you safe. The headquarters is the safest place for you right now."

Milan turns to Logan and tries to look around her dark sunglasses to see her eyes. She asks Logan about the whereabouts of David's body. Logan is quiet as she drives weaving through traffic caused by the explosion.

"Answer the question or stop the vehicle and I can get out here."

Logan looks around the car at their surroundings and pulls over.

"I can't do that."

Logan says and waits for a response from Milan while Milan stares at Logan in disbelief.

"Is he alive, Logan?"

"You watched him die, didn't you?" Logan says sharply.

"I don't know anymore. Why wouldn't his body be in the casket? Why were soldiers guarding an empty casket?"

"I saw what you saw. I wouldn't have thought to open the casket had you not insisted."

Milan gets out of the vehicle and places her backpack on her back. Logan reaches in the back and gives her a black baseball cap to put on.

"Don't look up."

Logan says as Milan places the cap on her head.

"I'm only a call or text away, don't hesitate to reach out if you need help. I can't give you the information you seek but I can protect you." Logan says.

Milan nods her head and shuts the door. She looks around inconspicuously as she scurries up the block away from the scene. She cuts through a few side streets to get to the main road a few blocks away and hails a cab. She avoids eye contact with the driver as she provides the address to her destination. Ten miles away in a neighboring town the car stops in front of a used car dealership. Milan looks at the meter and hands the man cash plus a generous tip. While on her way inside Milan scans the available cars and spots the car she plans to purchase. Milan approaches a man at the first desk she sees in the front office.

"I'll take the 2009 grey Camaro in the front."

Milan says as she places seven thousand dollars in cash on the desk in front of the man. The man says "ok" and pulls out a clip board with a few sheets of paper attached. Milan leans in close and places her hand on the stack of money.

"Off the books."

"No, I can't do that. We go by the book around here ma'am."

Milan adds three thousand more to the stack.

"For you."

She says as she slides and additional thousand dollars around the stack of money, directly to the man. The man shoves the stack of one-hundred-dollar bills into his pocket and puts the rest of the money in his desk draw. He quickly grabs the keys to the car and tells Milan to change the tags and plates within thirty days otherwise, this transaction will be void and the vehicle will remain property of the dealership. Milan thanks the man, grabs the keys and heads out of the front door. She rips the sale sign and company logos of the car. She adjusts her mirrors and programs the GPS on her cell phone to guide her to David's home.

After a few hours of driving Milan is alerted by GPS that she has reached her destination. She pulls up to a long winding road that leads to David's gated entrance. She slowly drives up, observing the property for activity. She reaches the gate and stops to search the envelope with property information to check for a key or code to entry. On the property map in the right-hand corner is a QR code with a numerical code directly below it. Milan scans the code with her phone and is prompted to type in a numerical code. A quick bright flash of green glares from her phone and scans her face. She remains still as she is caught off guard by the sudden flash of light. A thumb print pulses from the screen, so she places her right thumb on top of the screen. "Milan Brown" pops up on the screen followed by "security code accepted". The security system for the property is now at Milan's fingertips. Each dwelling on the property is listed on her phone's screen starting with David's main residence. All of the homes read "secured, system armed" next to a digital outline illustration of the properties. Milan pulls into the garage and takes a few minutes to learn the system application before venturing out onto the property. She finds the live feed security footage on the app and inspects the internal and external feeds for each property.

There hasn't been any sign of movement, so she walks to David's main house. Her eyes are drawn to the spot where she saw her father bleeding out during her last visit. The floors have been scrubbed clean and the place is spotless. Milan closes and locks the door behind her and walks around the main floor checking each room and exit points. All the windows are locked, and the place looks exactly the way it did when she was last there. She walks into David's office and sits in the chair at his desk. She spins around to face the window, gazing at the beauty of nature in his back yard. The wind blows and sweeps the fallen leaves around the yard and the rushing waters splash against the rocks a few yards from the property. For a moment Milan feels at peace, but only for a moment. Out of the corner of her eye, a black spider crawls on the beige wall to her right. The spider crawls inside the wall where there is no visible crack. Milan rolls the chair in closer and discovers a seam that extends from the floor to the ceiling. Upon closer inspection she discovers an additional seam about one yard from the other. Milan bends down and pulls up the edge of the carpet to inspect the base of the wall revealing a slit in the wall extending between the seams. She closes the window shades and proceeds to apply pressure on the wall. Once the right amount of pressure is applied to the right spot a door cracks open. Milan pushes the raised carpet down with her foot and opens the door. Two feet beyond the door is a silver metal door with buttons pointing up and down. She pushes both and the floor vibrates with movement coming from beyond the door.

Milan draws her weapon, stands to the side and braces herself for whatever lies ahead.

The door slides open to an elevator, Milan steps in without hesitation. She stares at the two buttons inside the elevator, one leading up and the other down. As the door closes abruptly, she hurriedly chooses the down arrow. Milan looks around the elevator for a secondary exit point. The shaft door on the ceiling is wide enough for her to climb through if need be.

She counts the amount of time she spends in transit in the elevator as it descends. After ten seconds the elevator stops, and the door slides open to darkness. Milan pulls out her phone and turns on the flashlight. She steps forward with her phone in one hand and her pistol in the other. As she moves forward the censored lights illuminate the room. A cave-like dwelling with doors carved into stone lies before her. As she walks toward the left of the room, she periodically turns around to watch her surroundings. Sleeping quarters with a bed carved out of the stone wall and black bed linens look untouched. The bed is made, and additional dark grey linens are stacked on the floor next to the bed. Milan sits on the bed and glides her hands over the duvet. The coldness beneath her fingers shatters her hope that her father may have cheated death. Milan proceeds to inspect the rest of the bunker. Parallel to the sleeping area is a small black refrigerator, a table and chair, and a cabinet filled with first aid supplies. A few feet from the makeshift dining area lies a locked black door. Milan tries all the keys on her key ring to unlock the door but none of the keys fit. She points her gun at the doorknob and prepares to shoot off the doorknob but decides to use the butt of the gun to knock the nob off the door. After a few swings the nob falls to the floor and the door opens.

Milan stands in the doorway in shock at the magnitude of explosives in the room. From floor to ceiling, blocks of C4 cover nearly every square inch of the small room. She closes the door and heads for another door at the end of the room. She opens the unlocked door to a wall with an exit sign ahead. To the left is a tunnel lined with censor powered lighting. Milan is light on her feet and leads with her pistol as she carefully makes her way through the professionally cemented tunnel leading to a right turn. A few yards in, Milan reaches a fork along her path. The path leading right is short and the daylight peers through the cracks in the cylinder-shaped door. Straight ahead, the path leads to an ascent for an unforeseeable distance. She turns right and slowly opens the narrow door to a large dip a few feet below the ground outside. The sun shines brightly through a sheet of intertwined twigs and leaves above. Milan pushes on the branches and they lift intact with ease. She pokes her head up through the hole and discovers she is in the backyard and directly behind the camouflage door is the rear of David's home.

Milan covers the hole, closes the door, and continues on her path to discovery. She walks back down the path leading straight through the tunnel and pulls out her map. She decides to walk to the closest stop on the map on foot. She Sets a timer on her watch and moves quickly while looking over her shoulder periodically. After five minutes of walking, she approaches a window built at a one-hundred-and-thirty-degree slant inward. Looking out, the view of the yard outside is slightly obstructed by branches and leaves. A few yards from the window along her path is an ascending spiral staircase and the tunnel continues at a right turn. Milan walks up the staircase and reaches a hatch door on the ceiling above the second flight of stairs. She slides a latch lock and pushes the door open. The sunlight surrounds a kitchen she walks into as she pulls herself up through the doorway. She looks at the map and discovers she is in the house David had built for her. Milan closes the door and slides a few feet away to the nearest wall and rests her body against it for a few moments. She looks around at all that her father built for her and is overwhelmed with gratitude. She would have had deep regret if she had cast her father off as a prodigal like everyone else.

Chapter 7

Reconnaissance

Milan fights back tears as she thinks about the violence and abductions she's experienced throughout her life. Coincidentally she was physically fit and prepared for each encounter. She believes she was guided by David, covertly throughout her path and eventual recruitment as an officer of the law. After her first semester in college Milan was bombarded by military recruiters, from tables strategically placed in front of her job sites and at her college campus to constant calls to her mother's home encouraging enlistment. She didn't see it then but, now she realizes the tact behind her being targeted.

After being chased off her campus and eventually abducted, Milan didn't feel safe enough to go back to school. She was vulnerable and needed a change of scenery. The constant presence of military personnel and their promises of security and benefits plagued her mind. Milan was cornered and needed a way to protect herself and get away. Joining the military seemed like her only and least expensive option at the time.

Milan excelled at basic training and advanced quickly. Her physical agility and her tenacity caught the eye of her Platoon Sergeant who encouraged her to pursue military police training. A few weeks after her basic training, Milan started a year long journey in Advanced Individual Training where she also excelled. A week before she was scheduled to take her Armed Services Aptitude Battery exam, she was barred from advancement and discharged from the military for inaptitude. Despite excelling during the gruesome training and being fully prepared to ace her exam, Milan was told she was not fit to serve in the United States military for failure to adapt to military environment. She received no further information and could not reach her Lieutenant or Commanding Officers.

Despite Milan's reason for enlisting in the Army, she developed a sense of pride in the thought of being charged with the duty of protecting her fellow citizens. She was running out of time and her next decision would determine the trajectory of her life.

Milan contacts Veteran affairs to gain access to her personal file. She submitted a military records request and was sent a letter stating there was no record of her ever enlisting or having been recruited. Milan's suspicion fueled her mission to discover the culprit behind erasing her record. She was sure someone effectively sabotaged her year of training, but Milan documented her journey. She stores all her milestones in a scrapbook and stores it, along with other memorabilia, in a decorative box. She went through all the photos in her collection until she found two featuring her Lieutenant and Commanding Officer. She snapped a picture of the physical photos with her cell phone camera and ran a search on google.

Lieutenant Aven Wilson and Commander Shyanne Brown were the names uncovered for the officers in the photos. After an extensive search of the two officers Milan had reached a dead end. She found it interesting that she and Shyanne share the same surname, Brown, but she brushed it off as a coincidence.

Milan walks through her newly inherited home, and across the living room to a large bay window with a built-in bench. She looks out at the compound and ponders her next step. This land has already been infiltrated and as long as she is alive holding such valuable intel, she will always be a target. The rest of her family could not rest with Legion on her back, at least not without cutting them off at the root. They have seemingly pervaded every branch of law enforcement and at least a portion of the military.

Milan sends Logan a text message asking her to perform a search on Shyanne Brown.

"Come to the headquarters and I'll show you how to access everything you need to know." Logan replied.

As Milan sits with her phone in her hand deciding what to respond, Logan sends the GPS coordinates from David's home to the headquarters. Although Milan did not inform Logan of her current location, she decides to rest her suspicions and assume this was the only address she had in connection with her. Milan responds to the message with a thumbs up and puts her phone in her pocket.

Milan worked through the night rigging the ditches and a few of the hidden entry points in and around the property with explosives. Each bundle of C4 has already been equipped with an electric battery that responds to digital signals transmitted to a lone source connector powered by a wi-fi connection. Milan connects the detonator to a touch screen application on her cellphone giving her the power to destroy the land and anyone on it during a security breach using her fingerprint.

By daybreak Milan awakens to the alarm on her phone. She draws the drapes in Davids's guest room and rummages through the packed closet for comfortable coordinates. She finds black hoodie and sweatpants to match, in her size. After a shower she finds a cannister of oats in the cabinet that has yet to expire so she makes a bowl of oatmeal and a cup of coffee. Milan found David's central video security system in his office. She reconfigures the feed to include the interior of David's home and office. The cameras facing the main gate of the property were turned off, so Milan secures the feed and heads out of the door.

Once at the headquarters Milan drives up to the rooftop parking garage where Logan greets her. Logan is stoic and hard to read. Milan doesn't know who to trust but figures she's made it this far she might as well proceed and see what is in store.

"Hello Milan. Follow me." Logan says as she leads the way through the building. Milan greets her with a hello and follows. They walk past the sleeping quarters and Milan remembers Paris, Lille and Marseille. She decides to wait to complete her solo mission before inquiring about the other ladies. Logan and Milan walk in silence until they reach double steel doors at the opposite end of the building. Logan presses her thumb on to a touch pad to the right of the door and a loud click follows. Logan pulls both doors open to a small room with multiple computers around an oval shaped desk with electrical cords hanging near the walls.

"The password is today's date. Perform your search in here until we get you set up." Logan says as she leaves the room and closes the doors behind her.

"Ok, thank you." Milan replies.

Milan types in the date in the eight-digit format and the screen transitions into four quadrants. The United

States Military on the top left, The Federal Bureau of Investigation, Central Intelligence Agency, and Internal Affairs Division, displayed clockwise. Milan looks around the room and directly into a camera to the right corner of the room and spots another one over her right shoulder. She hesitates for a moment and reminds herself that she "has a right to be here" and clicks on the U.S. Military screen. She finds a link on the site to locate military personnel and types in Shyanne Brown's name. *Military ID required* pops up on the screen. Milan reluctantly types in her ID number, 0615201614. The screen buffers for a moment and Shyanne's full profile shows up on the screen. Milan takes screenshots of all of the information including Shyanne's last known address. She performs a search on Lieutenant Aven Wilson and screenshots his information.

Milan's palms clam up and she starts to sweat before her next search. She cracks her knuckles forward and types in David Brown's name. His profile flashes for a split second before Milan's access is blocked by a *Classified, Access Denied* message displays in red across the screen. Milan closes the webpage at the sound of someone entering the room. Logan returns holding a laminated card with a string attached.

"Let's get you set up, so you have full access to the facility". Logan says and hands Milan her access card.

Milan accepts, closes the screen tab and follows Logan through a glass enclosed corridor to a connecting building. They walk into a large room filled with desktop computers and a large screen covering an entire wall. Milan walks behind Logan while looking back at the screen display flashes of various images and places. A few people sit in front of computers facing the screen manipulating the images on display. From monuments and historical sites around the world to military bases around the country, they have eyes in multiple places. Logan and Milan step inside of a cubicle in the back of the room. Logan stands before a computer and inputs information about Milan. She then instructs Milan to place her thumb on a keypad next to the computer.

"You'll have full access to the facility. Your thumb and or your face will be your master key. Certain parts of the facility will require you to scan your identification card however, classified regions will require your personal print." Logan says.

Milan complies. Logan pulls out a curved electrical device that is attached to the computer via a long USB cord. She places it in front of Milan's face and tells her to remain still while her face print is captured, and Milan complies.

"The headquarters will always be the safest place you will ever be. You can always return, and arrangements can be made to bring you back here from anywhere in the world. That goes for Paris, Lille and Marseille as well." Logan says.

"What is this place, exactly and has my father been here?" Milan asks.

"This is the place where the good guys come to retreat and regroup, those who have kept their hands clean. David stayed here often to heal and recover. The Doctor was his primary physician and the only one who he trusted with his health and you, of course." Logan shares with a smile.

"Did you find what or who you were searching for?" Logans asks.

"My father's file is classified. Why?" Milan asks.

"You father was a high-ranking government employee who was being hunted for years. It was for him and your family's protection." Logan replies.

"Why was he being hunted? What was he involved in?" Milan asks eagerly.

"Before you were born David and a few of his platoon mates discovered something sinister when he was promoted to Special Ops. Something that changed the trajectory of his life." Logan replies.

"What is his involvement with Legion?"

"He infiltrated the organization to get information. He is a great leader and even after they found out his motives, they tried to force him to stay, he refused and was hunted. That's why he stayed under the radar. He built his compound off the grid near the headquarters for this reason. His information was leaked. That's when he was ambushed." Logan looks at Milan as she stares into space.

"Keep digging. Some things you'll have to discover on your own. I think David left breadcrumbs because he may have wanted it that way to teach you to persevere." Logan adds.

Milan thanks Logan for the help, exits the facility and hits the road.

Milan drives bout twenty miles North of the headquarters and pulls up to a sign that reads United States Army Fort Melvin. She drives past the military base slowly looking for familiar faces as she passes by. Milan pulls up to a residential street three blocks from the base and parks. She calls Shyanne and requests a few minutes of her time to have an honest conversation about past events. Shyanne is silent for a moment before she reluctantly agrees to meet with Milan.

"I'll meet you outside of the base in fifteen minutes." Shyanne says, eager to get Milan off her back.

Shyanne pulls up behind Milan, gets out of her vehicle and looks inside at Milan through the passenger side window. Milan lets her in and cuts to the chase.

"What do you know about my father, David Brown?"

"I agreed to convince you to recruit." Shyanne replies sharply.

"Why?" Milan asks.

"To help you prepare for war against Legion." Shyanne says emphatically.

"Why was I discharged before given the opportunity to advance? I know it wasn't due to inaptitude because I was one of the fastest and strongest women there." Milan says.

"You were never meant to advance, only to train. At least not before all members of Legion were exposed. It wouldn't have been safe." Shyanne says.

"You and I sharing the same surname, is that a coincidence?"

Shyanne pauses for a moment then replies, "you father and I are third cousins through his dad."

"You failed to mention that to me when we were assigned to the same unit. How long have you known David?"

Shyanne looks around at the cars passing, in a paranoid manner. She is visibly uneasy and grows impatient.

"Is there someone out there who would have an issue with you speaking with me?" Milan asks.

"I gotta go."

Shyanne quickly exits the vehicle and speeds off in her own vehicle in the direction opposite the base.

Chapter 8

Reformation

Milan rises with the sun, anxious as she prepares for a mission that may cost her and her family their lives. She collects fruit and vegetables from the mini fridge in her room and places them on her small kitchenette table along with protein powder and a blender. After blending and drinking her breakfast she showers and stands in front of the mirror for a while, wiping the fog from her view. She takes in the moment to remember the woman she is now because her life may never be the same beyond this day. Milan pulls hair clippers from a basket beside her sink. She stands still with the clippers close to her head and hesitates for a moment. She then abruptly shaves her hair down to a buzz cut. She tosses the clippers in the sink and rests her hands on the side and hangs her head. She looks down at the floor covered with her hair and, regret sets in. "Am I making the biggest mistake of my life? Should I just hop on a plane now to Milan, Italy to finish this mission and move on. Move on to what? A lifetime of running from this group of bullies trying to dominate even the very forces assigned to protect the public.

How will there be any justice unless someone stops evil from permeating the land?"

Milan's mind races as she thinks back to her studies on behavior patterns. When dealing with perpetrators there was always a rhythm to their crimes and many of them continue to do harm simply because no one stops them. The satisfaction of evading capture becomes addictive, and the compulsion continues.

Milan paces the room as doubt and fear creep in. Her hands clam up and she sweats profusely. "It's now or never." She says before grabbing her backpack and leaving her room. In the main computer room, Milan accesses her personal profile in the system. She changes her home address to the address at David's compound. She logs out and leaves the headquarters.

--

Two days later

Milan sits in her car in the parking lot of the police station where she works. She puts on a wig with a bob cut and bangs, tinted metal rimmed glasses and adjusts her shirt and suit jacket as she gets out of her car. She walks in and offers a smile and nod to her colleagues sitting at the front desk. They stand in shock as they watch her walk through the front door. It had been months since Milan had been to her office and many assumed she left the force. She greets everyone in passing as if she isn't public enemy number one. She scans the faces of the people around her and takes note of their expressions. Surprise, dismay, delight, or anger. She takes note of everyone and everything.

She reaches her office and is met with a locked door. Her key doesn't work so she picks the lock with a paper clip. She looks around the room and almost everything is as she left it. Except for a new surveillance camera on the ceiling in the corner of the room. Milan waves at the camera and takes a seat at her desk. She spins around to face the door as multiple sets of feet move quickly toward her office. Sergeant Laura Simon leads the pack to Milan's office and stands in the doorway with a look of intrigue.

The rest of the pack stops at the doorway and Simon questions Milan as the others look on with mixed emotions. A couple of her fellow officers seem giddy to see her alive and back in the office. A few seem neutral while a few others who have already proven their disloyalty wear their anger with pride.

"Where have you been Brown? We didn't expect to see you again." Simon says.

"I'm sure you didn't, Sergeant. You too huh, Jacobs?" Milan says as the vision of her fellow officers turning on her plays over in her mind.

Jacobs stares at Milan and doesn't respond.

"Well, if there isn't anything else, I'd better get back to work." Milan says as she slowly closes her office door with Simon glaring.

Milan removes her jacket and places it on the back of her chair. She checks her file cabinets and snaps photos of a few documents on her phone and emails them to herself. She leaves her office and heads to the evidence room where Officer Jacobs is waiting and seething with anger. Milan doesn't see him standing around the corner in her blind spot. When she is out of view of others in the area Jacobs emerges and grabs Milan by her neck. He pulls her off her path and up against the wall he was hiding behind. Milan thinks of the multiple ways she will finish him but gives him room to tell on himself first. His fat hands swell around her neck as she tightens the muscles in her neck to prevent asphyxiation.

"Who told you to show up there? Why were you there, you messed everything up. We almost had her." Jacobs says as his eyes bulge out of the sockets.

"Who?" Milan says with a strained voice.

"The girl. You know who." Jacobs snaps back.

Milan takes a swift, hard jab into the creases of Jacobs elbows with her elbows while simultaneously kneeing him in his groin. Jacobs buckles from the pain as Milan swings him around by his arm and pushes him up against the wall. She uses all her might and kicks Jacobs in the face repeatedly until he is unrecognizable.

"For Paris." She kicks Jacobs once again causing his head to smash through the sheetrock into the wall. His body goes limp as he hangs, knees slightly bent with the wall holding him in place by his head. Milan looks over the blood-stained wall with an apathetic gaze before high tailing it out of the station.

Milan takes her time as she makes the trek back to David's neck of the woods. Feeling accomplished, Milan is calmed by the cool breeze blowing in. She tosses the wig and chuckles as she rubs her nearly bald head. She's still in disbelief about the drastic change but needed temporary freedom from the maintenance.

Back at the station, Jacobs is discovered, and Simon makes a call sending an attack on Milan.

"David is gone so you can kill her this time. Forget the chip." Simon says before hanging up the phone.

Milan is a couple of miles away from the headquarters when she receives an alert on her phone notifying her of activity at David's compound. Multiple censors have gone off at different points around the perimeter of the gate. Milan pulls up the security footage to find a fleet of black jeeps parked along the private road leading to David's estate.

Dozens of men climb the gate and draw their weapons as they approach the estate while a few remain behind near the vehicles. Most of the men are dressed in all black while others sport military camouflage pants with black t-shirts. The men disperse in different directions across the property using the target magnifier on the assault rifles to provide a bird's eye view ahead.

Milan texts Logan "We got'em, at David's place." While wearing a look of satisfaction.

Milan makes a swift U-turn in the opposite direction back to David's home.

Back at the Headquarters, Logan gathers the strongest and fastest soldiers available to finally complete the mission many of them have been pursuing for the past decade. She contacts the head of every security branch in the country to prepare for detainment.

Milan drives up to the main road leading to the compound. She parks her car under a willow tree and changes her heels and puts on a pair of combat boots. She secures a small pistol in one of her socks on her ankle, one on her side waist holster, one in her side shoulder holster and one on her waist band on the back of her pants. Milan looks around outside and secures a belt around her waist loaded with ammunition and a silencer attachment for her pistol. Milan puts on her dark sunglasses and gets out of the car. She gathers a few large branches covered with leaves to conceal her vehicle from view.

Milan walks along the shaded side of the road, out of view. She is shielded by the hanging branches of a willow tree on the side opposite the entrance gate. Seven men stand next to black jeeps that line the road in front of the gate. They actively keep watch of the main road and the compound as their cohorts invade. Milan crouches down and crosses the road making a b-line for the first man. With his back turned, Milan jumps up and wraps her arm around his neck pulling him down into a sleeper hold. The tall man is rendered unconscious as Milan slides him under the jeep he was guarding. She scurries up behind the next man and hits him in the back of the head with a large rock. She rolls his body into an upright sitting position and leans his body on the bumper of the jeep. The next man turns around and Milan takes cover behind his jeep. He walks around the vehicles looking for his comrades as Milan remains low to the ground as she stays out of sight. Before the man can reach his comrade slumped over the bumper, Milan slides under the jeep and trips the man causing him to fall to the ground. Dazed and confused, the man attempts to push up from the ground as the remainder of the guards come to his aide.

While under the jeep Milan draws her pistol and screws on the silencer attachment. She waits until all of the men have gathered within her line of sight and shoots each of them in the legs as they pass by. They fall to their knees in anguish confused about the origin of the shots. Milan rolls from under the jeep and on to the road. She quickly confiscates their weapons before they even notice her presence. Milan scurries behind a large tree on the opposite side of the road. She pulls out her cell phone and crouches down to the ground. She activates the explosives strategically placed around the property. She covers her ears and pulls her head between her knees to brace for impact.

The ground shakes as the earth parts to make room for the pressure from below. Fire shoots towards the sky and is swallowed by the lake rising to the surface. A stream long and wide is formed as the freshwater spreads throughout the compound. The guards' bodies have been strewn about the road from the impact. They are sprawled and lifeless as blood seeps from newly formed wounds.

The sound of multiple vehicles approaching the road pierces through the ringing in Milan's ears. A fleet of black jeeps approach and Milan locks eyes with Logan. They are mutually relieved to see one another. Logan jumps out of the jeep and Milan stands to meet her. A couple of helicopters fly over the property, one is the property of the United States Air Force and the other, an FBI military helicopter.

Men and women in dark colored suits pour out of the line of jeeps wrapped around the perimeter of David's property. Everyone stands and marvels at the men they had been searching for, for decades trapped on patches of land surrounded by a newly formed moat intertwined between the masses of land. The natural moat is deep and wide, leaving no opportunity for escape. The men stand helpless as they are ordered to drop their weapons as the officers have their assault rifles drawn from the air and land.

One of the men on the ground in a pool of blood from his gunshot wounds musters up the strength to look at Logan and Milan. Milan and Logan turn to look at the man trying to speak through a gurgle.

"The hydra has many heads, we are many. When we go away many more will rise. This is only the beginning. We are everywhere."

Milan and Logan look at one another seemingly unphased but inwardly exhausted. They hide their true emotions but remain silent and do not engage with the man.

Tear gas is dropped down to the cornered men. As they shout in pain and tend to their burning eyes, soldiers wearing gas masks descend with chains and hand cuffs and subdue the men. The high-ranking officers on land gather planks and lead the prisoners onto a court bus where their feet, hands and necks are shackled to the seats and floor. The men are transported to an unmarked federal prison a few miles away from the Headquarters.

The prisoners' electronics are confiscated, searched, and dissected and their vehicles are stripped down to the frames. Fingerprints and DNA are collected and analyzed within their universal database. A few of the men have ties to the military and have gone rogue or AWOL within the same time frame. The men are interrogated individually and remained tight lipped about the details of their criminal organization except for one. Logan stands behind the double-sided mirror and observes the body language of the men as they are questioned. The last man that is questioned, a young man, is led out of the room by a military police officer. He stops near Logan and the officer also stops to listen to what the man will say since he refused to talk during interrogation.

"The Hydra lives." The prisoner says to Logan as he walks by.

Logan and the officer share a look of concern before he leads the prisoner to the transport yard. The prisoners are loaded onto a few large transport buses and sent to a remote forever prison a few hours away in the middle of the dessert where they will remain until their natural deaths.

Chapter 9

European Tour

Milan, Paris, Lille, and Marseille hover around a large world map. Red markers are circled around the European cities they were named for. After weeks of planning and gathering supplies the ladies prepare for their European cruise to the coast of France.

Logan provided the ladies with aliases, phony passports, and Identification cards to travel abroad without being tracked. Logan drives the ladies five hours across state lines to board their cruise ship. The women wear wigs and board separately. Their rooms are on the same floor with balcony views of the ocean. They studied the blueprint of the ship taking note of all potential exits including their balconies if necessary.

Two weeks later the ship docks at the Coast of France.

"Welcome to Cannes France." The ship's captain announces over the loudspeaker followed by cheers from the passengers eagerly waiting to explore the city.

The ladies blend in with the large crowds with ease. By the time the four ladies deboard they are met with hundreds of ship passengers as well as thousands of attendees at the Film Festival reception taking place on the beach. Their trip was planned with the anticipation of a large crowd to further shield their presence on the continent. They bob and weave through the crowd with their oversized hats and dark sunglasses and head towards their meeting place.

The ladies disperse temporarily without acknowledging one another. Marseille heads to a bar on the beach, while Milan, Paris and Lille head to a small chapel a half a mile away from the beach, up a hill. Marseille is approached by a man who joins her at the bar. She puts her large purse on the seat next to her as the man closes in. He sits in the next available seat and looks around conspicuously. The mysterious man places a well wrapped, black plastic bag inside her purse and grabs a stack of cash nestled beside it. They never exchange words but mutual head nods instead. Marseille quickly unwraps the bag revealing two silver pistols, two black pistols, four silencer attachments and a few boxes of bullets.

Milan, Paris and Lille walk up different paths to the chapel. They meet inside and find the restroom. Marseille sends Milan a text letting her know about the exchange with the arms dealer and she heads to the chapel to meet with the ladies. The ladies change their clothes in the restroom of the chapel. Wearing business casual, they ditch the large hats and change wigs to compliment the new look. They each take a firearm and a silencer, and they divide the bullets evenly. They wrap their weapons in towels and nestle them at the center of their suitcases.

The ladies sit and wait while Marseille walks to the Cannes station about a half a mile away. She uses cash to purchase a one-way ticket to Marseille, France. Once she leaves the ticket counter, she lets Milan know her train will depart in thirty minutes. Paris and Lille walk to the station together. They arrive just in time for their respective rides to Paris and Lille France. Once Milan receives notification that all the other ladies have boarded their trains she walks to the station. Milan boards the train headed to Milan Italy. She has the longest journey of the four of them, so she uses her time to help them solve their riddles and complete their missions, starting with Marseille.

Marseille

Heroes and victims of the sea, below the gate there were three.

Milan checks in with Marseille to see if she has all that she needs for her mission.

"I already know what I have to do. I was prepared for this. The mission is in the sea." Marseille sends in a text to Milan. Milan reads the message, then deletes it to avoid being tracked.

Marseille refers back to her notes on the riddle.

"Heroes and victims refer to the lives lost during the First World War in the early 1900's. The monument at the Eastern Gate was erected to honor those lives. The monument is affixed to a boardwalk overlooking the sea." Marseille says quietly to herself.

The women have twenty-four hours to complete their mission to avoid run ins with Legion. Marseille exchanges her dollars for four thousand Euros before leaving the train station and books a night at a hotel near the Port that accepts cash. She drops off her luggage and heads to the Port to study the area. Marseille keeps her cell phone video recording discreetly as she walks to the monument.

She walks toward a green statue of a woman standing tall with her arms outstretched. Under the arch and around the statue lie engravings of the past. Marseille stops in her tracks and zooms in on an engraved message under the archway. *Heroes and victims of the sea, below the gate there were three.* Marseille nearly drops her phone as she reads the message. She looks around to see if she has captured anyone's attention. The streets are filled with passersby and two-way traffic, and everyone seems to be focused on reaching their destinations. Marseille continues down a set of great stone steps leading to a landing overlooking the Mediterranean Sea. The shore is a few hundred yards below and is covered in sand and smooth rocks of the same color. A staircase on the side of the landing leads directly to the shore. Marseille moves quickly down the stairs to the rocks below. She follows a path to the right of the monument that leads to an outdoor food court and a bar. The restaurants are built on large rocks that protrude onto the surface of the water. Underneath is clear green water with a view of the rocks and algae that extend from the shore to the sea floor.

Marseille sends Milan a text. "Diving gear", she writes.

A few moments later Milan sends her a list of four stores in the city that carry what she needs. Marseille rents a moped, travels to the closest shop, and buys a snorkeling set including a mask with a snorkel and headlights, a black wet suit, and fins.

Just as the sun rests on the ocean on the horizon Marseille gathers her gear in her backpack and goes back to the shore on the rocks. She finds a spot nestled in between a wall of rocks to change into her gear. She rests her cell phone upright, leaning it up against her backpack and presses record. Then, she gathers a few rocks light enough to lift and places them in front of her belongings, leaving room for her phone to record her movements. The waters are still, and the bar built on the rocks opens with live music. The people pour in, and Marseille makes sure she remains unseen as she descends into the deep waters. She has no clue where to begin but turns on her headlights and starts feeling around the base of the rocks lining the shore. The rocks vibrate as a man walks away from the bar and towards the shore. Marseille turns off her headlights and submerges her head under water and pulls in closer to the rocks. To her right, just under the base of the monument is an engraved message in fine script. She dives down deeper and quickly treads toward the sign.

Heroes and victims of the sea, below the gate there were three, the message reads. Marseille turns on her headlights and swims under the port. Three metal boxes are affixed to the large rock holding up the port above her head. She tugs on the boxes, and they do not budge. She slides the boxes side-to-side, and one is released. Marseille centers her light on the area and slides the remaining boxes out of the slide hangers they were resting in. The sun has nearly set, and the deep sea is growing dark. She turns off her headlights and checks the coast before climbing back onto shore.

Marseille's hands shake as she hurriedly changes into her dry clothes without drying off her body. She shoves the boxes into her bag and is in disbelief that this secret has been waiting for her, in this very spot, possibly since she was a child. She is nervous about traveling back to the hotel with who knows what is in those boxes. To avoid over thinking she walks briskly up the stairs to the moped. She puts on a brimmed fisherman's hat to help with her disguise.

Paris

A seat at the opera, twenty to be precise, to defend the Arche dessous, Triumphal Way.

It's 4:30 pm and Paris enters The Bastille Opera House for the 8 pm show. She shuffles through the crowd to the ladies' room. She has been rushing, bobbing, and weaving through life for the past year and hasn't stopped to enjoy the moment. She stops in front of a floor length mirror. The drape on her long black dress continues to flow as she stops. Her red lip pops through the dim lighting and her faux diamond studs sparkle and dance with the vanity lights above the mirror. Paris smooths down her sleek low parted bun and twirls her curls left out near her ears. She takes a mirror selfie before coming back to reality.

She brings up the notepad on her phone and memorizes her riddle before placing her phone in her purse.

Paris settles in her reserved seat, seat twenty. The lights in the room dim as the red velvet curtain parts on the grand stage. As soon as it is dark enough, and she is out of sight, she feels around her seat for clues or foreign objects.

A couple next to her becomes agitated after a woman misplaces something valuable. One of the theatre ushers approaches to assist.

"Regardez ci-dessous le siège." The attendee says.

"English, please." The woman responds politely.

"Look under the seat." The woman feels around and is relieved to find her diamond ring that slipped off her finger.

Paris hears the word dessous in French and is reminded of her riddle. She discreetly glides her hand around the bottom of her seat, then down to the base. She slides down to the floor and uses the flashlight from her phone to look around below her seat including the floor. She presses onto the floor with her hand in hopes of releasing a secret compartment in the floor. Paris eases back into her seat feeling defeated.

During the concert intermission Paris walks with the crowd out of the theatre. She sends a group text to the ladies asking for help solving her riddle.

"There can be many levels below your seat. Go to the next descending level and find the exact spot where your seat is located." Lille responds first and everyone else agrees.

Paris slips away from the crowd when she spots a staircase on her right blocked with a red velvet stanchion. She turns back to see if she is being followed, then steps over the velvet rope and rushes to the next level. She is met with a set of large double doors with a window on each of them. The doors are locked, and the windows are dark. Paris uses the flashlight on her phone to see into the dark room. Production supplies and chairs stacked to the ceiling offer Paris a glimmer of hope. On the right side of the room a winding staircase ascends to an opening near the ceiling of the room. Once up the stairs, Paris walks a few steps into a door on the left. She turns the knob slowly and it opens with ease. The room is lit and the few steps before her lead to a large crawl space that covers the space of the theatre. Paris closes the door behind her and removes her shoes before climbing the stairs. Once inside the sound of hundreds of footsteps fills the space from above. Her cell phone flashlight lights her path as she crawls through wires and debris. On the ceiling above are numbers. Directly above Paris' head is the number one hundred and as she moves forward, the number ninety. She proceeds until she finds number twenty. She can barely contain her excitement when she finds a black metal box nailed directly adjacent to the number twenty.

Paris finds a coin in her purse and uses it to loosen the screws and release the box. She glides her fingers over the numerical lock and contemplates whether she should just slip out of the theater unnoticed while she can or try and crack the code. She enters her birth date and to her surprise the lock is released.   The black velvet lined box contains a small envelope with a note card and a solid gold key within it and a black velvet pouch. The pouch fills the inside of the box. Paris releases the drawstring and opens the pouch. Her eyes widen and her face is illuminated by the brightness coming from the contents inside the box. She closes the box, shoves it under arm and quickly leaves the theater.

Back at her apartment rental, Paris changes out of her formal attire to something more comfortable. She closes all the windows in the apartment and draws the curtains shut. She puts the box on the bed and dumps out all the contents on the duvet. The raw blue diamonds retract light in a performative display creating an intricate dance between the facets and Paris' deep green eyes. Each cut has a unique shape and is reminiscent of diamonds fresh off the mine. Paris is mesmerized by the beauty of the rare stones. She turns and admires the tapestry of light covering all sides of the room. Sparkling Hues of blue and gold from the light fixtures remind Paris of a simpler time, the harmonious dance of ballet. Her mind races as she thinks of her father sitting in the audience cheering her on as her blue stone earrings cause the spotlight to cascade down to the crowd during her dance performance.

She reaches for her phone to call her father but hesitates. The risk of being found and taken again is too big a risk to take. Paris must solve the second part of the riddle and leave Paris, France within less than twenty-four hours.

Paris pulls the golden key and note card from the envelope. The note reads *Defend the Arche, Triumphal Way Twenty en Haut*. Paris does a deep dive into the words in her riddle, and they lead to historical landmarks. The Arch of Defense, also known as the Grand Arch and The Arc de Triomphe make the most possible sense since the landmarks are scalable from within.

Paris changes into an all-black casual pantsuit and puts on a black headwrap. She puts the pouch filled with diamonds in the freezer and the key and card in her crossbody purse. She stops in front of the mirror on her way out and decides her features are far too conspicuous to roam the town bare faced. She puts on a pair of oversized black framed glasses and a neck scarf she uses to partially cover her mouth and nose. Paris gets on her rented moped parked on the side of the home and heads to her first stop.

A five-minute ride into the city center leads to the main thoroughfare in Paris. Paris rides slowly down the well-manicured, tree-lined street called Avenue de la Grande Armée. The area is bustling with tourists marveling at the large statue towering over the city. She parks her moped out of the way in between two cars and crouches down out of view of the bright lights and scurries past two guards. The winding staircase within one of the arcs catches her eye and she walks briskly towards it. A few people gleefully walk up the stairs eager to reach the top for the view of the city. Paris keeps her cool to remain inconspicuous during her search. After traveling up a couple of flights she stops in front of a door on her left. The door is locked so she leans in closer to the door before trying her golden key for a fit. The key is not a fit and Paris keeps it moving, quickly up the stairs, skipping steps as she climbs. Just before the stairway leads to the rooftop Paris stops in front of a door with the number twenty engraved onto a golden plaque. She turns the knob slowly and the door opens to a small empty room with aged wooden floors. She steps into the room and closes the door behind her. The moonlight shines in the room through a small window in front of her. Paris feels around the walls and applies pressure into the floors hoping to release a hidden compartment or door beyond the barrenness of the frame.

The sound of feet rushing up the stairs near the door sends Paris into a state of panic. She falls to her knees and begins to dig into the spaces in between the floorboards and tugs. Finally, right before she reaches the wall near the window one of the boards releases with minimal effort. The space beneath the floor is hollow and dark. She uses the flashlight on her phone to pierce the darkness below. Among dirt and debris is a small plastic bag with Paris written across the surface. Paris hurriedly pulls up all of the surrounding boards that will budge revealing a manually dug small ditch layered with gravel and dirt.

Paris uses her flashlight to look for any other clues within the surrounding area before pulling the bag from the ditch. She opens the bag and pulls out a mini monocular. She stands to her feet and places it in front of her eye and stands facing the window. A microscopic hologram is hidden within the scope. A u-shaped building with partial blueprint coordinates of the west wing is engraved in green and blue. Paris recognizes the historical landmark, so she moves with haste. She replaces the floorboards and rushes up to the roof of the Arc. The roof is packed with people capturing the night lights within the city skyline. She maneuvers through the crowd with her monocular on her eye hoping the match the hologram with the monument.

The background noise is diminished by the faint words of a young woman standing in the crowd.

"Defend the Arche dessous for humanity". Paris turns around to a woman standing a few feet away bending over, close to the ground reading a message engraved in concrete. Paris discreetly weaves through

the crowd, making her way to the woman. By the time
Paris reaches the engraving the woman has found
solace in never knowing the meaning of the message.
At the center of the roof, standing at an equal distance
from the ledge on all sides, Paris leans up against a
cement post and reads the inscription. She puts her
monocular up to her eye and looks up at the skyline.
Straight ahead, down Avenue de la Grande Armée lie
the Arche of Defense. The building and the hologram
merge seamlessly as the hologram shines gold and the
twentieth floor is highlighted. A golden box is affixed
behind a wall within the crawlspace behind an office in
the West wing.

Paris has approximately thirty minutes before the
Grande Arche closes for the evening. Paris studies the
coordinates for a few moments before rushing down
the stairs. She hops on her moped and speeds down
Avenue de la Grande Armée. She parks her moped on
the side of the building and runs up the stairs leading
to the entrance to the reception area. The doorman
motions for Paris to come to the reception desk as he
notices her dismay once she spots the turnstile blocking
her path to the elevators. A woman wearing a trench
coat, business suit and heels steps off one of the
elevators. Paris zeroes in on the identification badge
hanging from the woman's neck. She waves to the
woman as she approaches. The woman is confused and
searches Paris' face for resemblance of anyone she may
know.

"Bon soirée" Paris says as she reaches over to hug the woman while simultaneously unclipping the woman's I.D. badge.

Paris quickly scans the woman's badge and walks through the turn style to catch the elevator before it closes. She sways from side to side, full of nerves as she counts the floors during the slowest ride ever, to the twentieth floor.

The doors open and the ceiling lights flicker as Paris steps out onto the dimly lit floor. She walks toward the first door on the edge of the west wing. Paris uses all her might to push, and kick open the locked office door with no success. She runs down the hall in the opposite direction jiggling doorknobs until one of the doors opens to a utility closet. Paris grabs the first couple of items she sees; a crowbar and a pair of scissors then scurries back down the long hallway. She stops and places her ear up to the door to listen for movement in the room. She places the sharp end of the crowbar into the frame and uses her foot on the other end to break the lock and pry the door open. The door slams open and Paris closes it behind her and heads straight for the wall on the opposite end of the room. She feels around the wall for unevenness or anything out of the ordinary. The floors squeak as she makes her way to the corner of the room.

The vibration coming from Paris' watch reminds her that she has ten minutes to vacate the building before it is closed for the night and silent alarms are activated. With a rush of adrenaline Paris rips the carpet from the base of the floors revealing a three-foot-long door with a golden keyhole. Paris marvels at the golden key before placing it in the keyhole for a seamless fit. With little time to process what is before her, Paris turns on her cell's flashlight and walks down a set of stairs. When she reaches the last step lights flicker on ahead. The passageway had been perfectly built into the floor with cement on all sides. She steps onto a path with a brick wall a few feet beyond, parallel to the entryway. The walkway extends to the width of the building with an additional hidden doorway on the East end of the pathway. A few feet above her head, a golden box is nestled in between the wooden frame. She uses the back end of the key to unscrew the box from the latch securing it to the wall.

With no time to inspect the contents of the box Paris runs to the opposite end of the pathway to investigate the other small, hidden door. The door opens to a long cement stairwell leading to an exit sign. The stairwell leads down a couple of flights before it ends at a door leading to the side of the building. Paris rushes back to the door in the floor and strategically flips the carpet over the door as she closes it and hopes everything falls back into place. She turns a manual lock on the hidden door from the inside before taking a chance on the unknown.

5 Minutes to spare.

Paris hesitates before closing the door behind her as she heads toward the exit sign. She double backs and the door has locked behind her. She left her borrowed tools behind and the only way out is through this doorway. Paris places the gold box in her backpack, rushes down the stairs and takes a deep breath as she grabs the doorknob hoping and praying the door will open. Paris holds her breath as she turns the knob. She lets out a sigh of relief as she pulls the door open and steps onto a narrow walkway. She walks carefully toward a round dark pit. As she steps forward censor lights begin to flicker on in a steady formation descending into what seems like an interminable bottom. The pit is lined with hundreds of metal ladder rungs leading to a two-hundred-foot drop. Paris looks around for any alternative routes out of the building. Her watch vibrates and reminds her she has 3 minutes to exit the building.

"God please help me keep my feet steady, help me to get out of this alive."

Paris says aloud as her body shakes in fear. She takes a deep breath, wipes the sweat from her head and rubs her sweaty hands on her clothing. She grips the first rung as she shifts her body down until her foot rests in the next one below. She moves at a steady pace and refuses to look down as she moves, gripping each rung tightly until her feet are steady, and grabbing the next.

Suddenly her foot slips out of place and her arm slips into one of the rungs catching her fall. Paris hyperventilates and hangs on for dear life as she catches her breath. She looks up and can see how far she has traveled, then she looks down realizing she is at the halfway mark. She moves quickly hooking her whole arm into the rungs securing her grip.

The countdown begins as her smart watch counts down from sixty seconds. Her feet touch the bottom at the three second mark. She uses the full force of her body to push open the metal door at the bottom a few feet from the ladder. Paris makes it out just in the nick of time. The cool breeze from the night air hitting Paris' face is like a comforting wind from the gates of Heaven. The door shuts behind her as she falls to her knees and catches her breath. She looks around for witnesses and the few people out for a night stroll hadn't noticed her presence.

Paris gathers her bearings and realizes she is at the South end of the building. She calmly walks around to the front and hops on her moped and heads back to the apartment.

Lille

Exchange the keys for twenty-four homes of old on display. A pointe of Paris where victories we will celebrate.

Lille has spent the entire trip to the city of Lille, France deciphering her riddle. After hearing of the treasures uncovered during Marseille's mission and the convoluted path taken during Paris' eventful mission, Lille is thrilled for the hunt. She walked through each location of the mission the day she arrived in Lille. She captured images of the artifacts she had been assigned to retrieve.

She takes the five-minute walk from the Lille Flandres Railway train station to the Old Stock Exchange at the Lille City Center. She enters the large courtyard surrounded by pillars and archways and joins the bustling crowd of people buying and selling in the open-air market. She blends in and buys a Keychain with her name on it and keeps it moving. Lille attempts to mask her excitement as she pulls her shawl over her mouth to shield her beaming smile as she weaves through the crowd. She stops at the twenty fourth archway and stands before a wood lined vintage glass case carved into the wall. Inside lies an antique brass skeleton key nestled in a red velvet lining. Lille marvels at the key for a moment before swiftly stabbing the glass with a cutter, piercing through the case. The glass remains intact as she pulls the display from the case and swipes the key. She pulls up the velvet lining and feels around underneath and pulls out a piece of paper folded into a small square. Lille places the glass cover back into place and removes her tool with ease. A small hole and star shaped crack go unnoticed by busy patrons as she slips out of building.

Lille rents a moped and helmet and takes a ride down Rue Pierre Mauroy Lane to Porte de Paris, ten minutes away. She parks under a low hanging tree where she reads the note, pulled from the display case.

A key for the Kings quarters, above the shrine lie living waters.

Lille memorizes the words before walking across the street to the historical building at the center of the small town. Tourists fill the small patch of land. They gaze at the tall, preserved structure and the intricate detail marking the history of the city. Lille walks through the building which is a mere six feet in length from entry to exit. She stands in confusion as she searches for the rest of the building.

"King's quarters?" Lille says as she walks around the structure.

On the opposite side of the building beyond the pillar arches is an old wrought iron gate lined with spikes with a *Do Not Enter* sign affixed to the side. Lille puts on her shades and fakes a selfie, inconspicuously checking her surroundings for any onlookers. She puts her cell phone in her backpack and scales the gate, carefully climbing over the spikes. Lille steps onto an open space with a brick wall and a door sized plank of wood nailed to the center. She wastes no time, pulls out a pocketknife, and unscrews the four nails holding up the plank. She checks her surroundings once again and places the plank on the side of the wall, revealing a vintage brown door. She pulls out the skeleton key and places it in the keyhole and jumps for joy as she turns the key and unlocks the door. Natural light peers through the frame of a door on her right. Lille uses the light from her phone to find the doorknob. The keyhole is reminiscent of the first door, so she tries the skeleton key once again. As the lock clicks open, she simultaneously turns the knob and wastes no time running up a short set of black, shiny steps to the second level of the narrow building. Lille remembers the circumstances surrounding her visit and ducks as she passes the window on her right. She peeks out as she crawls up the steps and gets a full view of the front of the building and part of the city center.

She is amazed as she walks into the open room. The walls are draped in red velvet with gold trim, traditional golden Louis XIV baroque chairs covered in red damask brocade fabric rest against the walls, and original artifacts from King Louis XIV's conquest fill the alley shaped room. Above a long floating shelf on the wall is an old painting of the Deûle River with a message in gold drawn over the river.

He that believeth on me, as the scripture hath said, out of his belly shall flow rivers of living water.

Lille carefully removes the painting from the wall and some of the paint lifts with the painting. She peels a patch of chipped paint revealing a sheet of cardboard. She quickly peels enough of the paint to pull the cardboard away from the wall. A perfectly carved square shaped hole with a small, black safe lay before her. She carefully pulls the safe out of the wall and places it on the floor without making a sound. Lille places the painting back on the wall and puts the safe in her backpack. She snaps a few photos of the artifacts in the room as well as a close up of the painting. As she steps in closer to the painting, she notices a set of numbers nearly microscopic in size at the base of the river where the water meets the foliage beside it. She uses her camera phone to zoom in closer to the numbers, it's her birthdate written in six digits starting with the day. She snaps the photo and heads for the doorway, walking on tiptoe as she leaves the room. Lille locks both doors behind her and moves the wooden plank back into place in front of the main door. Lille waits for tourists and passersby to move out of view before scaling back over the fence and heading back to the moped. She hops on, puts her helmet on and looks back at the building, feeling a sense of adrenaline and satisfaction for having completed her assigned task.

Lille returns her moped and heads back to the train station to catch the next train back to Cannes. Lille arrives back on the coast as the sun sets and the lights from the festival illuminate the beach as party music blares through the city and Film Festival goers celebrate their accomplishments for the year. The cruise ship remained docked as some passengers have chosen to sleep in their rooms on the ship and avoid the large crowds and added fees from hotels on the beach.

Lille is the only one of the four ladies who did not spend the night in her assigned city. Lille stands on a hill overlooking the action below. She is at a crossroad. One path leads to fun, drinks, music, local food and camaraderie, while the other leads back to the ship. As Lille walks back to the ship she remembers the treasures in her backpack, the possibility of being found and potentially blowing the mission. She puts some pep in her step as the excitement of the discovery intensifies. She has yet to try using the number sequence she found on the painting to see if the safe will open, or if extreme measures will need to be taken to crack the code or the safe itself.

By nightfall the women gather in Paris' room to crack open their boxes and reveal their findings together. They place a sheet on the floor, sit in a circle and lay all of their treasures on the sheet. Paris' proudly spreads her blue diamonds before her as the ladies marvel. She used a pair of scissors to pry open the second box, a golden box filled with gold chunks and nuggets. Lille uses the code she captured on the river painting to open her box which was filled to the brim with perfectly polished white diamonds. Marseille excitedly revealed her collection of polished and raw cut canary yellow diamonds. Along with their treasures they read the notes they received among the treasures.

"A good man leaveth an inheritance for his children's children, and the wealth of the sinner is laid up for the just. – Proverbs 13:22"

The Third Day

It is 9:00 am on the third day of travels and Lille, Marseille and Paris anxiously wait for Milan to make it back to the ship. The ship hatch will be closed by 9:45 and will depart at 10:00am sharp. The ladies have been calling and texting Milan throughout the night and have yet to receive a response. All the ladies were to complete their missions between the first and second day of deboarding the ship. The plan was for each of them to return to their rooms on board at different times by the second night to leave room for mishaps or entrapment.

Paris, Marseille, and Lille pace across the upper deck overlooking the shore and the road leading from the train station. They contemplate staying in Canne as the clock strikes 9:40 in case Milan needs help. However, the next ship arrives in thirty days, and they are unable to risk blowing their covers by traveling by plane. Paris calls Logan and asks for direction on their next move.

"I'll find her, stay on the boat." Logan says.

At 9:45 the captain blasts the ship's horn as it moves from the shore. The ladies stand on the deck in silence and wait and watch until the shore of Cannes, France is no longer in view.

Chapter 10

Nothing But the Blood

"David? David!"

Milan screams at the top of her lungs while walking toward the Arch of Peace in Milan, Italy. The man watches Milan from afar and does not react to her yelling as she runs in his direction. The man stands calmly until Milan is within a few yards from the Arch and he places a black box on the ground and walks out of site. Milan picks up the box and runs, shouting David's name, searching frantically for the strange man.

Four Italian police officers point in Milan's direction as she walks around the courtyard dazed and frantic.

"Signorina, rimani dove sei!" (Miss, stay where you are)

One of the officers shouts while walking closer to Milan with his hand resting on his pistol in his waist holster. Milan realizes they have directed their attention to her, and she turns around to gauge the distance between where she stands and a gateway to another part of town. She quickly scans the area for a train station, warehouse, alley way or a large crowd of people. She looks forward and tries to pick up on any Italian words that may be familiar. She backs away from them and continues to walk backward until one of the officers snatches the box out of her hands while another swings her around and places her in handcuffs.

"What is my crime? I haven't committed a crime! Why am I in handcuffs?!"

Milan shouts, intentionally drawing attention to herself from onlookers.

"Tu hay sconfinato nel Castello di Castelprio." The officer says while securing the cuffs.

"What does that mean? In English, please!" Milan turns to look at the officer and speaks.

"You where trespassing at the Castle at Castelprio."

"The castle is open to the public, officer. I haven't done anything wrong."

"The castle is closed for construction; didn't you see the sign? What where you looking for, ma'am?"

"I don't speak Italian, I didn't know. Release me from these handcuffs. This is unlawful imprisonment." Milan tries to remain calm as her mind races to figure out a plan of escape before her true identity is exposed.

Milan endures a five-minute walk of shame as she is escorted by police to a small station just outside Sempione Park. Milan's cell phone along with the contents from her pockets are removed and confiscated. Her cuffs are removed, and she is placed in one of two jail cells in the station as the officers attempt to open her box. Three of the officers gather around the box to investigate. Milan cringes in her jail cell as one begins to shake the box causing the contents to rattle inside.

"Attorney!" Milan yells from her cell.

A processing officer approaches Milan's cell and asks her for her identification. She tells the woman she doesn't have any identification on her but, if she can call her attorney, she can get the information for her. The officer looks at Milan suspiciously and walks away. The officers converse among one another in Italian. Milan picks up on the word "Spiare" mentioned during their conversation.

"Spiare? No spiare! I am not a spy, I'm a tourist. Turista." Milan says.

"You do speak Italiano?" The arresting officer says with sarcasm.

I know a few words, but I am not fluent, and I have no ill intent. The officer offers a smug shrug and continues to attempt to pry open Milan's box.

Two Days Ago

A bridge in the Alps over the Simplon Pass, a road to Paris through Jupiter's Gate. When Roman walls fall Cagnola will rise triumphant to find a place for Castelsprio's fate.

Milan books a cash only hostel room and pays for two nights up front plus a security deposit. She puts her backpack in the closet, grabs her map, a pair of dark shades, a small set of binoculars, her cell phone and heads out the door. Milan keeps the video active on her phone as she walks to Jupiter's Gate, seven minutes from the hostel. She holds her phone discreetly at her side while periodically pulling it up to her face, faking a selfie to confuse any admirers.

The medieval structure is packed with tourists and a group of children on a class trip to the historical site. Milan walks through and captures video of as much of the building as she can, both inside and out. She hasn't the slightest clue what to look for and parts of the building are sectioned off with caution tape and are guarded by Military personnel. One of the guards spots Milan through the crowd, locks eyes and nods. She captures the man on video and continues to walk through the crowd, watching him from her peripheral as she passes by. He never takes a second look and offers no such acknowledgment to any other visitor.

The crowd of people are directed through the center of the building, to the enclosed courtyard and through the exit. Everyone must walk in the same direction. People are free to linger as long as they'd like, however no one can double back through the entrance. Milan captures as much footage as she can, zooming in on every window, door and walkway in the courtyard. Milan leaves the heavily guarded site and takes the rest of the evening to comb through photos and video footage to prepare for her next move.

The following day Milan rents a moped and take a thirty-minute ride to Castelsprio Park in Northern Italy. She pulls up to the Grande Roman Castle. Half of the tall structure is dilapidated with the main entrance draped with yellow caution tape. Milan walks around the seemingly deserted property and finds a small opening in the building beyond a pile of stones. She checks her surroundings, turns on the video on her phone and bends down to enter the building. As soon as both of her feet touch the ground a silent alarm is instantly triggered and faint red laser light field forms in the room around her. Milan remains still and scans the room to find four camera bulbs concealed in the corners of the open room. The open sky above, the small doorway from which she entered and the path ahead to the unknown are among the available options out of the room. Green lights turn on, on the surveillance cameras and rotate toward Milan. She backs out of the room and the red lights flash. Two cars pull up to the front of the castle and the sound of stern, rushing footsteps follow. Milan runs behind a large tree and sticks around to see which uniform shows up to the scene. Military personnel along with men wearing black suits walk through and around the building. Once they search the empty building and look around the premises, they reset the alarm and leave the area. Milan just so happened to park her moped near a bush, placing it out of view of law enforcement keeping her out of dodge.

Back at the hostel, Milan changes her clothes and puts on a baseball cap and continues on her mission to the Arch of Peace where a seemingly familiar man leaves behind a black box.

The Third Day

Milan wakes up in her jail cell the following morning at the sound of a woman asking about her. The woman used the name on Milan's fake passport, Patricia White. Milan squeezes part of her face through the bars to see who the woman is. A short, middle aged woman with ash brown, shoulder length hair stands at the processing counter. The woman, dressed for business steps within Milan's sight, locks eyes with her and winks before alerting the guards that she has come to bail her out.

"Sí, agente, é lei." (Yes officer, that is her) The strange woman says as she points to Milan.

A male officer Milan has never seen opens her cell and tells her she is free to go. Milan walks out of her cell and cautiously toward the processing desk where the woman is standing.

"Milan Brown I'm Doctor Warren, come with me." The woman whispers.

Milan leans into the processing area and spots her box under a stack of papers. She grabs her box and looks through the sheets of paper. Photos and still video shots of her around town including the Castle at Castelsprio and Jupiter's Gate. She takes the papers with her as the guard locks the cell and follows Dr. Warren out of the building. The doctor leads Milan to a charcoal grey Ferrari. When the doors shut Warren informs Milan that Logan found her when the Italian military sent out a Green Notice to retrieve information on a woman fitting Milan's description.

"We have to get you out of Italy, now." Warren says sternly.

They stop by Milan's hostel, and she quickly gathers her belongings. They hit the road and embark on a two-hour drive North through the Simplon Pass. The doctor glances over at Milan, who is quiet and offers some insight.

"Don't worry all you need is in that box. And of course, your blood."

Milan looks around frantic for the vial of blood given to her months prior by the Doctor at the Headquarters.

"Not to worry, I'll collect more. The vial was filled in case something happened to you during your journey. We needed to ensure that we had at least some of it so you could change the world even in your absence."

Dr. Warren says with a proud smile.

"Change the world?" Milan says, confused.

The smile leaves Warren's face. "You don't know what you have in you, do you?"

"I don't know what that means, David was always so secretive about everything. What do you know about my father?"

“I know you’ll find out a lot more once you get that box open and I show you what your blood is comprised of.” The doctor says.

Welcome To Switzerland.

A sign appears as they drive around a steep curve into a mountain range with quaint-looking, old-fashioned homes nestled throughout. Milan pulls out her cell phone to capture the beautiful landscape but realizes her phone is dead. Then a gut-wrenching feeling sinks in as she remembers Paris, Marseille, and Lille and how worried they must be when she didn’t show up for the return trip in Cannes. Milan lays her head in her hands and attempts to calm her racing mind as she wonders about their safety.

“You’re worried about your girls? Logan is in contact with them they’ve been informed about the plan. You were never meant to travel back the same way you came. You’ve always had a different path.” The doctor says.

Milan listens intently and has come to realize more has been kept from her than she thought. However, she decides to reserve her questions for a later time.

They pull up to a cream and brown colored cottage with evergreen colored window shutters. The garage has been built into a large rock that extends to an open grass field with homes sitting a few acres apart. Warren leads Milan through a door connected to the home and down to the lower level. The steel walls and motion censored doors are reminiscent of an aseptic medical facility. They walk into an office with mahogany wood furniture throughout. The egress windows adjacent to the door provide a clear view of the garage and the main road in front of the home. Dr. Warren invites Milan to sit on one of two seats in front of a large desk at the center of the room and Warren sits across from her behind the desk.

Milan asks for a pair of scissors, a phone charger, and other tools to open her box and Warren obliges. Warren leaves the room for a few moments and returns with a wheeled cart with the supplies Milan requested as well as medical tools and sterile gloves. Milan collects her tools as Warren sits at her desk to prepare for a blood specimen collection from Milan. Milan picks the lock on the box and slowly opens it, anticipating an unlikely surprise like a cranked box with a jack waiting to pop in her face.

Two black velvet pouches, one short one long, along with a United States Military badge with an embroidered military name patch resting on top.

"P. Caldwell." Milan reads the name on the patch out loud.

Dr. Warren lays her tools down on the desk, removes her glasses and shares the story of Sergeant Major Caldwell.

"Seargent Major Pearson Caldwell is a respected Veteran who worked with your father in the military. He is the longest survivor of stage IV pancreatic cancer, and we believe your blood will cure him. And all cases of cancer. Your blood is so rare it doesn't even have a category."

Dr. Warren says and waits for a response from Milan to avoid overwhelming her.

Milan stares blankly and is at a loss for words.

"Ok." Milan says, in such a way that Warren feels encouraged to proceed.

"I don't mean to be so graphic or intrusive, but have you noticed unusual color during your menstrual cycle?"

"Well, sometimes my blood will be a normal shade of red with some purple every other month or so. But I always thought that was normal until I overheard my parents discussing it as if it were abnormal. But they never mentioned anything to me about it. My father just drew some of my blood from my arm himself and I never heard anything else about it." Milan says, eager to hear more.

"David shielded you from a lot and made sure you knew how to fight for a reason. I believe he effectively hid you blood anomaly among other things, but we need to get this ball rolling just in case I'm wrong."

"I am an Oncologist and a Clinical Laboratory Scientist, and I have been researching and testing for a cure for cancer, specifically pancreatic, for the past twenty years. I would like a few samples of your blood so we can save the world together. Is that ok with your, Milan?"

Dr. Warren says with a smile.

"Yes, let's do it." Milan says as she removes her jacket and rolls up her sleeve.

Warren rolls her cart over to Milan and sits in the seat across from her. Milan extends her arm as Warren ties a tourniquet around her bicep. She lays three vials on the tray and disinfects Milan's arm before sticking a butterfly needle into the crease of her arm. Dr. Warren is amazed as red blood with streaks of purple fill the glass tubes.

"In all my years, I've never seen anything like it." She says as her eyes grow wide.

"How often do you get sick, cold, flu, or anything else?"

"I've never been sick as far as I can remember." Milan says.

"Wow, You a special lady." Warren says with excitement.

Milan smiles silently but is eager to get back to her box.

"I shall return." Dr. Warren says as she smiles at Milan with admiration and pushes the cart and specimens out of the room.

Milan pours the contents out of the small pouch. Bright red, raw, natural rubies spill out into the box along with a small scroll tied with gold ribbon.

"She is more precious than rubies, nothing you desire can compare with her -Proverbs 3:15." The note reads.

She opens the second pouch and pulls out two long bricks of solid gold along with an additional tied scroll. *"A good man leaveth and inheritance for his children's children and the wealth of the sinner is laid up for the just – Proverbs 13:22"*

David has never been much of a religious man but any and everything good, he was willing to show and share with his daughter.

At sound of footsteps, Milan quickly shoves the rubies and gold back into their respective pouches, closes her box and puts the box into her backpack.

Dr. warren hands Milan an envelope.

"This is your ticket for your flight. It's a semi-private flight so, no security screenings, I'll drive you directly to the plane on the tarmac. We should get going. You'll be flying back home out of The Swiss airport." Dr. Warren says.

Dr. Warren takes the scenic route to the airport which also happens to be the most secluded from public view.

"I feel it's only right you know why this mission was so important." Warren says. Milan perks up in her seat.

Warren shares how she and Milan, Paris, Lille and Marseille's father met over twenty years ago. Warren was a Military Physician when she met the fathers. She was working in the lab when she learned of the deception of some of her fellow cohorts in her unit. Their lab was trusted as one of the most secure in the country. A few members who worked in her lab, along with Field Army personnel joined forces with an anarchist militia group to have open access to United States pharmaceutical components. They were offering to pay a large sum of money to enact biological warfare, and the unprincipled soldiers took the bait.

David was propositioned by another rogue, affiliate gang in his unit to work with spies and pay for Intel about the countries within the European Union. Instead of joining the group he, along with the other three fathers planned a heist and stole the jewels that were presented as payment for intel. The payment boxes were presented to the dirty officers empty. As a result, a few of the members of the gang, now known as Legion, were killed. David was the ringleader and has been on their hit list ever since.

"David and I ran into one another when we realized we were up against the same forces. We worked together to foil their entire operation. He did his part, and I did what I had to do in the lab to protect my research and the country. No one ever knew I was one of five who foiled their plans, leading the dirty officers into a war against one another. Well, they were disorganized, it was pretty easy, actually. But I decided to retire out of the way and stay off the radar, just in case."

Milan listens quietly as all she ever wanted to know is revealed. She remains silent but relieved to finally know the truth.

Once the truth has been shared, both Milan and Dr. Warren feel a sense of relief as they ride through the plush valleys and untouched mountains through the small town. The roads are bare, and the skies are clear. Milan closes her eyes and remains present as the clean, cool breeze brushes through her short curls.

"Beautiful, isn't it?" Warren says as she glances over at Milan.

"Perfection." Milan offers a smile and thanks Dr. Warren for her help with everything. She assures Milan that she enjoyed the adventure and was delighted to help.

Thirty minutes later they arrive at the small airport and Warren pulls up to the tarmac. She stops in between two other cars dropping off passengers. Milan and Dr. Warren say their goodbyes and Milan joins the handful of passengers boarding the plane. Everyone on the plane shares a look of old money or new influencer wealth, nothing else in between. Milan finds a seat near a window and breathes a sigh of relief. She puts her bag on the floor under the seat in front of her with one of her legs inside the straps, keeping it stationary. She lays her head back on the head rest and closes her eyes. Someone sits beside her. She turns to look and covers her mouth to hold in a potential scream.

"David!" She says before jumping over to hug him. She sits back into her seat to get a better look at his face and pinches his cheeks to make sure he is truly present. They both chuckle.

"You did good kid." David says.

The End.